"Oh!" ... *her stomach and wanted for the baby to flutter again.*

"What's wrong?"

Rather than answer she reached for his hand. Pulling it toward her, she felt him tense.

"It's okay."

Laying his huge, warm hand against her stomach, she covered it with her own. The baby didn't keep them waiting long before a well-aimed nudge from inside pushed at their hands. Nick's gaze flew to her face and she saw her own wonder and excitement mirrored in his eyes.

Realizing the intimacy of the gesture, Faith removed her hand from his and looked away. She cleared her throat before speaking. "I thought you should be one of the first to feel it move. Thank you for sharing this." She felt heat climb up her neck and settle in her cheeks. "It makes it seem more real to share it."

He didn't answer, but his hand rested more firmly on her middle, molding itself to her belly—as though he had been touching her forever.

READY FOR BABY!

When parenthood takes you by surprise!

Will they…?

Won't they…?

Can they…?

The possibility of parenthood: for some couples
it's a seemingly impossible dream. For others,
it's an unexpected surprise…. Or perhaps it's a planned
pregnancy that brings a husband and wife closer
together…or turns their marriage upside down?

One thing is for sure, life will never be the same
when they find themselves…ready for baby!

THEIR MIRACLE BABY
Jodi Dawson

TORONTO • NEW YORK • LONDON
AMSTERDAM • PARIS • SYDNEY • HAMBURG
STOCKHOLM • ATHENS • TOKYO • MILAN • MADRID
PRAGUE • WARSAW • BUDAPEST • AUCKLAND

ISBN 0-373-03766-X

THEIR MIRACLE BABY

First North American Publication 2003.

This edition published by arrangement with Harlequin Books S.A.

® and TM are trademarks of the publisher. Trademarks indicated with
® are registered in the United States Patent and Trademark Office, the
Canadian Trade Marks Office and in other countries.

Visit us at www.eHarlequin.com

Printed in U.S.A.

CHAPTER ONE

"YOU can't be serious, Mr. Burns." Faith Kincade clenched her jaw in frustration. "The conditions surrounding the conception of my baby are confidential." Her hand fluttered across her still flat abdomen. "I'm not sure I understand the need for Mr. Harrison to be present during this meeting."

This isn't happening. Her nightmare was becoming reality.

Turning her back on the attorney, Faith walked with stiff dignity to the wall of windows on the far side of the upscale office. She brushed the bangs from her eyes with a weary hand and swallowed the soft sigh that nearly escaped her lips and replaced it with a fortifying breath. There was no option, except to deal with whatever came her way next. As she had every day since the accident.

"Miss Kincade, I assure you that Mr. Harrison's presence is a legal necessity." Mr. Burns shot her a look that fell just shy of being apologetic. "He is the only sibling of your late brother-in-law we have been able to contact, as well as being directly affected by the contents of the will…"

His voice droned on in legalese as Faith felt the last ounce of blood drain from her face. A will made it final. She forced herself to focus on each word coming from the lawyer's mouth.

"I will conclude the reading as swiftly as possible." Mr. Burns cleared his throat and looked directly into her eyes. "Whatever information you choose to reveal to Mr. Harrison concerning the conception of the child will be up to you."

The rustling of papers on his desk signified an end to the conversation. She turned her gaze on the scenes below the window, hoping to escape reality for a few brief seconds with the view of downtown Denver.

It offered no illusion of escape.

The morning that had begun washed in watery sunshine had matured into a gray-capped, heavy sky. Aimless snow fell onto the heads of people rushing by on the sidewalk. Anyone glancing upward could easily catch a glimpse of her face, but no one bothered to raise their gaze from their shuffling feet. Faith felt the relentless isolation press closer. If not for the precious life stirring within, she might be tempted to surrender. But the baby gave her a reason to fight.

The attorney acted in accordance with Steve and Carrie's wishes in carrying out the terms of their will. Verbally attacking the man wasn't like her, but Faith hadn't been acting like her true self for several weeks.

Truth be told, she admitted her anger was ultimately directed toward Nick Harrison. More than anger—undiluted rage. Though she'd never met the man, she'd hoped to never lay eyes on him. The heartache he had caused her sister and brother-in-law by his selfish actions was unforgivable. Nick Harrison turned his back on his brother and had never met Carrie. Now he would never get the chance to know how special his brother's wife had been.

Although Nick wasn't directly responsible for the car accident, Faith held him accountable. The less he knew about Carrie and Steve's child, the safer she would feel.

Reality came rushing back with the insistent buzz of the intercom atop the massive desk. The indefinite present thrust at her with all the finesse of an avalanche.

Mr. Burns answered the summons instantly. "Yes, Ms. Walters?"

"Mr. Harrison to see you, sir. Shall I send him in?"

Rather than respond, he looked across the room at Faith.

What did he expect her to do? Scream like a banshee and hurl herself in front of the office door to keep Nick Harrison out?

It was better to face the situation than to fear the unknown.

Clasping her hands together to steady them, she nodded to let Mr. Burns know she was ready.

Show time.

Mr. Burns pressed the intercom. "Send him in, please."

This was it—no delays and no turning back. Shuddering, she turned to face the door, feeling her life was about to irrevocably change. Struggling to maintain an air of detachment sapped her nearly depleted reserve of inner strength. The heavy, wooden door swung open on silent hinges, blocking Faith's view of the man who entered.

Nick Harrison approached the attorney with long, purposeful strides, each step proclaiming his confidence and power. Awareness of him as a man raced through her traitorous body.

Until she focused on his face.

Shock caused the breath to wedge in her throat.

My God...he looks so much like Steve.

Exhaustion put Nick on edge. What he wouldn't give to be tending the mares at the ranch. Hauling wheelbarrows of manure held more appeal than this stuffy office.

"Thank you for coming on such short notice, Mr. Harrison." Mr. Burns picked up a file from his desk. "I hope your trip proved uneventful."

Nodding his reply, Nick turned toward the woman. Her attempt to remain in the background caught his attention more effectively than if she'd shouted. Delicate and pale, she looked ready to collapse. Silhouetted against the gray skies beyond the windows, she might have been sculpted of stone. Except for her eyes.

Raw, sapphire ice pierced him. It seemed he'd acquired an enemy before he'd opened his mouth. She had to be Faith Kincade. No warm family welcome here, as if he'd actually expected one.

He had questioned her need to attend the meeting, but Mr. Burns simply answered it was necessary. No explanations. In Nick's experience, secrets usually meant trouble.

Mr. Burns stepped toward them. "Allow me to introduce your sister-in-law, Faith Kincade."

Nick's narrow-eyed gaze cut off the rest of the introduction. The reminder of family ties only served to emphasize that they no longer existed. He didn't need any words to do that, the heaviness in his soul reminded him daily.

Nick offered his hand resignedly. "Miss Kincade."

It was evident she wasn't going to raise her arm.

Letting his hand fall to his side, he angled his chin upward. No handshake? Fine by him. She obviously viewed meeting him as less than a joyful family reunion. Another man might have crumbled under the animosity of her gaze, but Nick decided to let her get over it.

Turning away, he shrugged. Her attitude wasn't his problem. The ice queen was welcome to nurse the chip on her shoulder—alone.

A movement out of the corner of his eye captured his attention. Accustomed to moving quickly, instinct spun him toward Faith when she swayed. Seizing her upper arms, Nick steadied her. She looked ready to shatter in his grip.

"Don't touch me." Faith's voice emerged low and calm. A far cry from the turmoil Nick read on her face.

Nick released her arms, surprise overtaking him before the emotionless mask he'd learned to wear replaced it. *Okay, time to cut this short.* He turned to Mr. Burns and set things in motion. "Can we get on with this?"

The lawyer rubbed the back of his neck, obviously stressed by their open hostility. Nick spared no more than a flash of pity for him—this was the man's job. He crossed to the desk and sat down. Things kept going from bad to worse, why should this meeting be an exception?

Motioning Faith to the remaining chair, Mr. Burns opened the file he held and contemplated the contents.

Nick held himself upright, braced to hear whatever followed. A glance in Faith's direction showed her motionless and pale in her seat. Her profile betrayed the strain she seemed to be feeling. Chestnut brown hair swept forward and concealed her from his bold gaze. She was a puzzle. Nick didn't care for puzzles—he preferred straightforward answers.

He shifted his attention to Mr. Burns and dread settled in his gut like a boulder. The shaking of the attorney's head didn't bode well for what they were about to hear.

Mr. Burns raised his attention from the file, looking first at Faith, then turning his attention to Nick. Long seconds dragged by. Audible ticking from a nearby clock stretched Nick's patience almost to the snapping point. Mr. Burns fidgeted.

Finally the attorney's voice broke the silence. "When drawing up a will...most young people do not consider the situations that may be produced should the document become necessary." He paused. "I am certain this was the case with regard to Steve and Carrie. Please remember, they had no way to foresee the complications this document might cause both of you."

That said, he proceeded to read the will, his reading glasses perched on the bridge of his nose. "I, Steven Lee Harrison, do hereby bequeath my share of the Whispering Moon Ranch to my child."

Nick stiffened. "Child? Steve didn't have any children." He glanced at Faith. What did she know about this?

She ignored him and remained silent.

Pushing the glasses higher on his nose, Mr. Burns cleared his throat. "Mr. Harrison, if you will allow me to continue, I believe the situation will be clarified."

Nick looked from Faith to Mr. Burns, confused. Estranged or not, he knew Steve would have told him if he'd fathered a child. God, he hoped he would have.

He nodded at the lawyer. "Finish it."

"If the aforementioned child is not of legal age at the reading of this will," Mr. Burns sent an enigmatic look at Nick, "the shares will be held in trust by the birth mother. Faith Kincade shall also act as on-site trustee at the ranch."

Agitated, Nick turned to Faith. Her stunned gaze focused

on a point beyond the lawyer's shoulder and her eyes reflected the shock running through his veins.

"What the hell is going on?" Nick demanded. He didn't like where his suspicions were headed. He willed Faith to face him. Slowly she turned her head and he tried again. "I want to know what's going on." *How can she be the birth mother?*

Faith placed a slender hand over her stomach in a protective gesture. Jutting her small chin forward, she looked him square in the face.

Gutsy. He'd give her that—Faith wasn't intimidated. And she didn't keep him in suspense.

"You're going to be an uncle." She blurted then clamped a hand over her mouth as the wide eyes of a cornered animal looked at him above her fingers.

Nick felt his disbelief give way to disgust. Bile rose in the back of his throat—bitter and metallic. The protective gesture suddenly made sense—she was pregnant with Steve's baby. Distaste rushed through him. Unable to remain seated, he pushed himself out of his chair and towered over her.

"Did your sister know?" Revulsion dripped from his words.

She held his gaze. "Yes."

Nick found no guilt or remorse on her face. "You're telling me she died knowing you carried Steve's child?"

"Yes." She pressed her lips together.

Ignoring the lone tear that slipped beneath her thick lashes, Nick ran agitated fingers through his hair. *This is unbelievable.* He'd thought he was beyond being shocked by anything people did, but this stunned him.

Nick leaned over Faith's chair and rested his hands on the armrests. "How could you sleep with your sister's husband?" He pushed the question through clenched teeth.

"Circumstances surrounding this child, my child, are not your business." Finger's tangled in her lap, Faith continued. "I will not discuss them with you."

He struggled to hold his temper in check and spoke inches

from her face. "Like hell it's not. The minute my ranch became involved, it became my business."

"Your ranch?" Faith's tone goaded him.

That's what she's after. Nick shook his head in disbelief. "You conniving—" Anger crowded the words out of his mouth. "This looks like a nice setup to you. Maybe you won't have to work another day in your life."

She met his gaze evenly. "I support myself, Mr. Harrison. You're out of line."

"Line? Woman, you're so far out of line it might as well not exist." Her gall amazed Nick. "You're not fit to be a decent mother."

Faith recoiled as if he'd physically slapped her. Nick raked his gaze over her and searched for signs of her condition. He scanned her from head to toe and, finally, focused on her stomach. A Harrison baby grew there. He had to focus on that—it was all that mattered. Pushing away from her, he faced the attorney.

"How does this affect my ranch?" Nick ignored Faith's startled gasp. He couldn't worry about her, only Steve's child.

Mr. Burns's gaze bounced between them. "Mr. Harrison, if you'll be seated…"

Nick returned to his chair. Deep breaths weren't helping to stem the rage rising in his chest. How could he not know about this? Again, he confronted the attorney. "Did you know about the baby? Why wasn't I told?"

"I am bound by client-attorney privilege." Mr. Burns paused and seemed to consider his next words carefully. "Due to the unique nature of this situation, I have consulted several family court judges. I will present your options as clearly as possible."

Nick released the breath he'd been holding. His future might very well hinge on the lawyer's next words.

"Miss Kincade is, of course, the child's legal guardian. The law encompasses the child's inheritance under this designation." He glanced at the papers spread on his desk. "To preserve the child's interests, the court would likely deem the best solution to be for Miss Kincade to assume her position as on-site trustee at the ranch.''

Nick swore under his breath. *No way is this going where I think it is.*

Faith addressed the attorney. ''Is there another option?''

''Possibly. But the court proceedings could extend interminably. This is the most workable solution,'' Mr. Burns answered.

''Workable for whom?'' Faith perched on the edge of her seat. ''I have a business to run, a life.''

Nick watched her shoulders sag. He resisted an urge to soften toward her. She and his brother's hormones were the reason they were in this mess.

''I'll contest it.'' Nick's statement seemed to put the fight back in Faith.

''Contest it? You'd take the birthright from your brother's child?'' She stood with fists clenched at her sides.

Ignoring her question, he uncoiled himself and stood to face her.

She tipped her head back to meet his glare and poked his chest with her finger. ''No one messes with this baby, especially you.''

Startled by her attack, Nick found his gaze focused on her parted lips. Her breaths came in irate puffs and anger brought a flush to her cheeks. He opened his mouth to retaliate.

Mr. Burns stopped him. ''Mr. Harrison, Miss Kincade.'' The standoff was suspended. ''This is bringing us no closer to a solution.''

Nick shoved his clenched fists into his pants pockets. *Solution, my eye.*

Faith stalked to the windows.

She addressed the attorney in a brittle voice. ''What is the best option for the baby?''

''Based on extensive research and considerable thought—''

Nick's harsh grunt interrupted the lawyer.

Ignoring him, Mr. Burns continued. "The court would look favorably on any action taken in the best interests of this child. Miss Kincade's establishment of residency at the ranch would certainly be considered a positive action."

Faith flinched and panic replaced the anger in her eyes.

Nick squashed the pity he wanted to feel for her and confronted the attorney. "It won't work."

Mr. Burns eliminated alternate routes of escape. "Until, and unless, the two of you can agree on an equable solution, it will have to."

Nick reverted to desperate tactics. "What if custody of the child is contested?" The question left a rotten taste in his mouth. *Think of the child.*

Faith turned her dismayed gaze to him, but he refused to back down. The future of Steve's baby demanded he leave personal feelings out of the situation.

Mr. Burns removed his glasses. "I'm not certain I understand what you are asking."

"What if the court determined Miss Kincade to be an unfit mother?" Nick didn't look in Faith's direction. He concentrated his thoughts on his brother's unborn child.

"I'm the mother." Faith's voice wavered. "You have no right to suggest something like that when you don't know anything about me."

"Through your own admission, you're pregnant by your sister's husband." He ignored her sharp gasp. "That, alone, speaks volumes about your suitability as a parent."

Mr. Burns rolled the chair back from his desk and stood. Beads of moisture shone on his upper lip. "Now see here…that is quite enough, Mr. Harrison. Slander is uncalled for. This baby—"

Faith gestured sharply with her hand, stemming the attorney's words. Nick watched as the two exchanged glances.

Something's not right.

"Thank you, Mr. Burns." Faith's gaze swung to Nick and stayed there while she addressed the attorney. "What's the bottom line?"

Nick's eyes narrowed. *I'm missing something.* He waited for the man's response.

"Miss Kincade, I believe it will be in the child's best interests for you to accept your appointed position at the ranch." Mr. Burns paused. "I must caution you both, a legal battle for custody of this child could be decided either way if based solely on the information provided at this meeting."

The undercurrents masked in the attorney's words added to Nick's confusion. He forced himself to concentrate as Mr. Burns turned to him.

"Mr. Harrison, I believe you desire what is best for your brother's child. A custody battle would prove lengthy and unpleasant for both you and Miss Kincade."

Nick contemplated Faith's grim profile. There was no choice to be made. The welfare of Steve's baby had to be his main priority and having Faith at the ranch would ensure he'd be able to keep tabs on her.

"I'll go to the ranch." Faith's voice was firm.

Nick hadn't expected her to surrender so readily. He'd obviously underestimated her determination. Or maybe, her greed.

"I won't change my mind about fighting for custody," Nick challenged.

"Are you threatening me, Mr. Harrison?"

"Promising. I want you to know exactly where you stand." Nick crossed to her and stared into her upturned face. "I always win."

Faith didn't flinch. "I don't scare easily. Shall I follow you, or would you like to draw me a map?"

CHAPTER TWO

DECEITFUL women, invariably, wear the face of an angel. Nick guessed it was Mother Nature's twisted sense of humor. He didn't find it amusing.

Frustrated, he pressed his foot down on the accelerator. The southbound, rush-hour traffic only increased his sky-high tension.

Faith's wide eyes and pale face forced themselves into his thoughts. He knew better than to be fooled by an attractive face. After his mother's abandonment, he figured he'd have learned his lesson by now. Apparently not.

The sun slipped behind the mountains and reduced the foothills to smudged outlines. He might have appreciated the rugged view yesterday. Today, it merely existed.

Nick slammed his palm against the steering wheel. Losing Steve had been hard enough—there was no way he would lose his child, too. He concentrated on relaxing the viselike grip of his driving hand. Cramps in his fingers reminded him that the pressure he inflicted on the wheel had been punishing from the moment he'd turned the key.

Weaving through the heavy traffic, he put the city farther behind him and the ranch closer. He needed to think. Calmly and rationally.

Yeah, right.

Faith Kincade had managed to have the last word. She'd thrown his challenge back in his face and was coming to the Whispering Moon Ranch. What was he going to do about it?

Damned if I'll welcome her with open arms. He'd tolerate her presence only long enough to find a legal way to boot her out on her shapely bottom. And a way to keep the child. He owed it to Steve and to the mess their family had become.

15

This child belonged on Harrison land and deserved to know where its father came from.

Nick had been surprised by how young and naive Faith appeared. If she fastened her hair in a braid, she could easily pass for a teenager. Her flawless skin emitted a fresh, scrubbed look. *Damn.* He suppressed his body's instinctive response.

What the hell were you thinking, Steve? Obviously his brother hadn't been thinking, only acting.

All impressions of young innocence had vanished when he'd slammed into the hostility in Faith's eyes. Antagonism that bitter was usually hard won. He wondered how he'd earned it? But more importantly, he wondered why it mattered?

Driving by pure instinct, Nick hashed his options out in his head. He thought through every scenario possible, but none of them were realistic or workable.

Forty minutes later, he headed west. Rubbing his aching eyelids, he concentrated on the narrow road. Winding uphill, it deposited him at the gates to the ranch.

Closing the gates behind him, Nick shook his head ruefully. Steve was gone, but he'd left an unborn baby behind. He was too exhausted to analyze his feelings. Family relationships obviously weren't his strong point.

Nick and his two brothers had drifted apart following their mother's abandonment. He now realized just how far apart. For the first time in weeks, he wondered where Logan might be. It wasn't that he didn't care—it was simply easier to distance the uncertainty and pain. His youngest brother had abandoned the ranch only months after Steve left for college.

As far as he knew, Logan still hadn't heard of Steve's death. And Nick didn't have a clue how to locate him. The detective he'd hired to trace his brother had come up empty. It was as though he'd never existed.

Nick stomped the brake pedal as a more immediate problem sprang into his mind. The force of the abrupt halt jerked the seat belt taut against his chest. Gravel spewed from the tires when he accelerated again. He couldn't keep up with everything he needed to keep track of.

Events had raced forward so fast at the attorney's office, Nick hadn't taken time to consider the logistics of Faith's arrival. Where was he going to put his unwanted visitor?

The original ranch house, occupied by his foreman's family, was full. He wouldn't ask Wayne and Mab to shoulder his burden. Explaining the circumstances surrounding Faith's presence would be tough enough. *How can I explain something I don't understand myself?*

Putting Faith as far from him as feasible seemed imperative. He wanted contact kept to a minimum, and he was certain she wanted the same. The master bedroom was on the main floor. That was about as far as he could place her from his rooms on the second floor, without putting her in the barn.

Nick hadn't entered the room since his father's funeral. God knew what kind of grime was there. A year was a long time for a room to sit empty, but it would serve her right to stay in the musty room.

Who am I kidding?

Nick sighed. It wasn't about Faith Kincade. She carried a Harrison baby in her slim body. Circumstance demanded he treat her decently, or as decently as possible given the situation.

Ed Harrison had drilled, and occasionally beaten, good manners into his three sons. He had demanded they act like gentlemen at all times. It had been his misguided attempt at making them well-rounded men. Still, Nick couldn't ignore a lifetime of discipline.

He knew Mab would insist on preparing the room. She'd probably dance a jig at being given the chance since she'd been after him for months to clean out his father's things. Seemed she'd finally get her way, she usually did.

What was he getting into? More precisely, what had Steve dragged him into?

Nick had exactly one month to work it out before Faith Kincade arrived at the Whispering Moon Ranch.

*   *   *

Faith laughed. The sight of her best friend, Laura, sitting atop the overstuffed car trunk was hilarious. Bouncing once more, her friend managed to latch the lock. The final bounce sent the petite woman sliding off the car, only a bit of fancy footwork saved Laura from landing on her back.

Faith was grateful for the opportunity to laugh. "If you could only see yourself. Too bad my camera is packed."

"I still don't like this." Laura straightened, wiping dirt-smeared hands on her jeans. "What do you know about this Nick character? Other than the fact he ignored Steve?"

"I have to think of the baby. Steve and Carrie wanted the baby raised at the ranch if…anything happened." Apprehension raced along her nerve endings and she shivered.

"Sure, but—"

"I'm going. It's not forever, just long enough to figure out what Nick is up to. Maybe I can convince him to drop a custody fight." Her tone discouraged further discussion. "Any more questions about the store or house?" She was relieved to have the bookstore in her friend's capable hands. As the assistant manager at the store, Laura knew everything needed to operate the business. "Let me know when they finish redecorating your condo and I'll make other arrangements for the house." The pieces had fallen neatly into place. As though she were destined to go to the ranch. Or doomed.

Laura followed her into the house for a final walk-through. "How can you think you've forgotten anything? It's all in the trunk."

Faith smiled. "I think you're right. I can't believe I thought it'd be a cinch to pack the bare essentials." She wrinkled her nose in vexation. "I'm just not sure how long I'll be there…"

"What'll I tell Devon if he asks about you?"

Faith glanced at the pale line on her ring finger. Relief coursed through her. The engagement ring she'd worn for nearly a year was gone. Once she'd committed to carrying the baby, Devon had changed his mind about their upcoming marriage. *Thank heaven.*

"He won't ask," Faith assured, "It's been months since we called off the engagement—he's moved on."

Laura looked skeptical. Faith glanced once more at her checklist. It confirmed the pointlessness of putting off the inevitable. It was time to leave. The sooner she arrived at the Whispering Moon, the sooner she could come up with a solution to the aggravating situation.

Laura enfolded her in a gentle hug.

I can't do this. Faith knew she didn't have a choice. She held tight, clinging to the security her friend offered.

Stepping back, Laura wiped her eyes with the back of her hand.

"Stop that," Faith commanded, "I'll only be three hours away, not three days."

Walking arm in arm, they approached the crammed car. Faith slowly lowered herself into the driver's seat. At six months pregnant, her balance was becoming precarious. *Amazing the difference a month makes when you're pregnant.*

"Thanks for everything, Laura. I'll be fine...really." She didn't know which of them needed the reassurance more.

"Just remember you're not a prisoner. If he doesn't treat you right—come home."

Faith honked as she pulled away from the curb. The map Nick had tossed at her a month ago lay on the seat beside her. She picked it up and confirmed the directions then merged smoothly with the southbound traffic on the highway.

She glanced once more at the map dangling from her fingers. The broad strokes and lines on the paper symbolized the hostility Nick had shown following the reading of the will. *Like I had any way of knowing what Steve intended.*

It still seemed unreal. Steve and Carrie must have drawn up the will as soon as the pregnancy was confirmed. Organized to the brink of perfectionism, Carrie would have insisted on it.

And here I am.

She'd been prepared to despise Nick Harrison, but the first glimpse of his face caught her off guard. The likeness to Steve had been fleeting—no more than obscure details. As a whole, he looked nothing like his brother. Steve had looked like a bookish professor. Nick was a rancher, from the top of his sun-streaked hair to the tips of his scuffed cowboy boots. Comfortable in his skin and confident of his place in the world.

If she encountered him as a stranger on the street, Faith admitted, she'd definitely give him a second look. Pregnant or not, she still had eyes in her head. His rugged good looks and barely restrained sexuality combined into a potent package.

Why can't he look like the toad he is?

Frustrated at the turn her thoughts had taken, Faith gave herself a mental shake. Nick Harrison was public enemy number one in her book. Remembering that was vital to her peace of mind and to keeping the baby.

Droplets of rain spattered the windshield, forcing her attention to the traffic around her. The last thing she needed was to wreck her car.

Once she arrived at the ranch, the vehicle would ensure she wasn't trapped there.

Three hours later, Faith rolled her shoulders forward trying to relax the tensed muscles. The gates to the ranch were directly in front of the car and she didn't relish a run in the rain to open them. Some welcome—not that she'd expected anything different. She peered upward at the leaden clouds, but they showed no sign of stopping their deluge anytime soon. She resigned herself to dodging raindrops.

Ah, springtime in the Rockies.

Faith zipped her jacket to the prude level and pushed her door open. The wind-driven rain drenched her in seconds.

Chilled, she faced the weather and placed one foot into the mud.

Stepping gingerly onto the surface of the slick road, her

shoes became sodden lumps. Thick mud built on them with each plodding step.

Faith reached for the gate. One moment she had her fingers wrapped around the latch, and the next she lay flat on her back blinking raindrops from her eyes. Her feet had slipped and her temple throbbed where she'd banged into the gate on her rush to meet Mother Earth.

Her initial instinct was to rise up out of the cold mud. Sitting upright, Faith gasped as searing pain streaked through her right side. Pinpointing the exact location of the pain was impossible. But Faith knew she had to get to the house— now. A bump on the head was one thing, possible injury to the baby, another.

Staying dry wasn't an option. Any body part the rain had missed was now plastered with mud. She grasped the slick rails of the gate and, painfully, pulled herself up.

Hunched over, Faith fumbled with the latch and pushed the gates open. She stumbled toward the car. Using the hood to keep herself steady, she made her way to the open door and eased her backside onto the seat.

Please, God, let the baby be all right.

Shivering, she forced her shaking hands to grip the steering wheel, but couldn't feel the leather under her palms. Dizziness and light-headedness threatened to overcome her. There was no time to sit and feel sorry for herself—every second might make a difference for the baby. She turned on the headlights to penetrate the gloom. Twilight had descended while she'd wallowed in the mud.

Passing beyond the gate was a major milestone. *No way am I closing it.* A glimmer of light through the pines pinpointed the location of the house. *Almost there.*

Faith tried to control her quaking, but it was pointless. The heater blast didn't warm her. She needed dry clothes and something hot to drink.

Finally the house came into view. Darkness shrouded the details, but the glow of lights beckoned through the windows promising warmth, if not welcome.

Jerking the car to a stop, she didn't bother to shut it off. Focused on the front door, she limped to the porch steps. Each step caused the throbbing pain to deepen. The hand she placed on the rail seemed to belong to someone else.

Step up. Pull on the rail. Step up. Pull on the rail. Step up.

Three steps conquered. Now, cross to the door. Her feet refused to cooperate but it didn't matter. Shuffling would get her there just as well. If only the ringing in her ears would stop.

Footsteps sounded behind the door. Good. Faith didn't relish standing in the cold all night.

Can goose bumps get goose bumps? Faith laughed at her cleverness. She was feeling warm and fuzzy.

The door swung open and bright light outlined her rescuer. Faith stepped toward the figure with outstretched arms...and slipped into the welcoming blackness.

Unbelievable. Nick stared down at the sodden mess draped in his arms. The lady sure knew how to make an entrance.

Swinging Faith's slight weight against his chest, he kicked the front door shut. With one arm around her shoulders and the other under her knees, Nick cradled her as he would a child. *How in the world did she get herself in this condition?*

Wet hair lay dark as midnight against her pale skin. Smeared with mud, she still managed to look delicate. Nick shook his head. Faith Kincade was about as delicate as a spring blizzard and twice as cold. One meeting had taught him that. Looks were deceiving. The phrase was becoming his mantra.

Nick headed toward the master bedroom, pushed the door open with his boot and crossed to the bed. Lowering Faith onto the quilted spread, he then pulled a blanket over her. The mud would wash out—it was important to get her warm.

A strand of hair clung to the fullness of her lower lip. Without thinking, he reached down and brushed it aside. Lightning raced up his arm from the contact with her soft flesh. Startled, he jerked back.

Damned libido picks a hell of a time to kick in.

Unnerved by the intimacy of the gesture, Nick turned and picked up the phone.

Time to call in reinforcements.

CHAPTER THREE

MAB arrived five minutes later. She kicked muddy boots behind the kitchen door and shed her dripping raincoat. Her worn medical bag was swathed in plastic. Efficient as ever.

Relief shot through Nick like adrenaline—Mab would know what to do. He silently congratulated his foreman on having the good sense to marry this woman.

She was all business. "Where'd you put her? Any change in her condition?"

"Dad's room, I haven't checked on her since I called you."

Mab dismissed his last comment with a wave of her capable hand as she hurried down the hallway. Nick followed—unsure what she expected him to do. *Shoot, show me a lame horse and I can figure it out.* An unconscious, pregnant woman was way out of his realm of experience.

Faith hadn't moved. Mab gently pulled the blanket down. She raised her eyebrows when she saw the mud on Faith's clothes and turned question-filled eyes to Nick.

He shrugged. "I'm as clueless as you are." He walked to the window and scrutinized the darkness. "She rang the bell, babbled, then passed out cold. My guess is she fell opening the gates."

"Why didn't she just buzz the house?" Mab removed Faith's sodden jacket and jerked her head in the direction of the muddy shoes.

Nick assumed he'd received his orders and moved to the foot of the bed. "Guess she didn't notice the callbox." Caked mud hindered his efforts to remove Faith's shoes.

"How far along did you say she is?"

Nick froze. The socks he'd removed dangled from his fingers. *Steve's baby.* "I'm not sure, several months. You don't think—"

"Now don't get worked up, I haven't finished my examination yet." Placing the earpieces of a stethoscope in place, Mab placed the business end inside the neckline of Faith's shirt.

Nick turned and occupied himself by rummaging for towels in the closet. He wasted ten minutes refolding each shelf of linens individually. The suspense ate at him. Finally he turned to see Mab shining a penlight into Faith's eyes.

Faith squeezed her eyes closed against the glare. She groaned and twisted her head to the side. Mab nodded, seemingly reassured by the reaction.

"I'm a nurse, not a doctor. But I'd say our patient has upgraded. Sleeping, instead of unconscious." Mab placed her equipment back into the medical bag. "A small bruise on her forehead and no signs of spotting. We'll keep an eye on her, but I don't feel her abdomen contracting. For the moment, miscarriage doesn't appear to be a threat." She pushed the hair off Faith's forehead. "Judging by the mud she has on her side, she's gonna have a whopper of a bruise. Plus a touch of hypothermia that can be controlled with warmth."

Nick felt the tightness in his gut unwind. A knock on the head and hypothermia explained Faith's bizarre behavior. He hadn't realized how tense he'd been. For the baby, of course.

"She'll need a change of clothes. Can't have her catching a chill along with everything else." Mab's deft fingers unbuttoned Faith's shirt.

Nick swallowed hard. Damn, she couldn't expect him to stand around while she stripped the woman naked. "I'll see what I can come up with in her car."

Seconds later, he shoved a worn Stetson onto his head and stepped outside. The cool night air seeped through his shirt in seconds. He sucked deep gulps of the moisture-laden air into his lungs and felt his balance return.

Even asleep and looking like a half-drowned cat, Faith Kincade managed to rattle him. Nick liked to be in control—

he prided himself on it. What was it about this woman that worked its way under his skin?

Sound penetrated the part of his brain still on track. The rumbling of Faith's car engine struck a discordant note. The pounding rain almost drowned it out. Nick loped to the car, his shirt drenched before he reached the driver's door. He reached in and killed the engine, then pocketed the keys.

Peering into the back seat, he found what he needed. Pulling the large suitcase over the seat, he grabbed the smaller one next to it.

I'm not making another trip out in this rain.

Nick hurried back. Standing just inside the front door, he wiped the mud from his boots and shook the rain from his hat. Mom would be proud. *Yeah, right.* Some habits were just hard to break.

Picking up the bags, he headed to the bedroom. Nick dropped them and knocked on the wooden panel of the door.

"Come on in." Mab's muffled words stopped him cold before he pushed the door open.

He didn't want to see Faith again. Not yet. Especially if Mab had managed to remove the rest of the wet clothes. He'd just slip the bags in, head to the kitchen, and grab a cold beer. *Good plan.*

Mab yanked the door open and pulled him inside the room by his shirtfront, obviously not thrilled with his hesitation.

"For heavens sake, Nick. Did you think I'd put the poor girl on display?" Mab grabbed the smaller bag and turned away.

Nick saw the quilt tucked primly under Faith's chin. *Good.* A pile of clothing lay in a heap next to the bed. A scrap of lace topped the pile like a dollop of cream. Her bra. Tension radiated downward. He whirled on his heel and watched Mab rummage through the bag. She pulled a flannel gown out and waved it in the air triumphantly.

"Perfect, glad to see she's a sensible girl." Mab approached the bed. "How 'bout some coffee. I'll be finished here in a couple of minutes."

Nick gave a gruff nod and headed for the kitchen. If he had to use kitchen duty to escape the room, he'd take it. But scooping coffee grounds and boiling water weren't having the effect he'd hoped. His mind continued to wander back to the bedroom and the scrap of lace masquerading as a bra. Images of the flannel gown slipping across bare skin and Faith's dark hair spread across the pillow taunted him.

He slammed the spoon onto the countertop. Wayne was right—his foreman had been after him for months to get out more. Date. Nothing serious, just someone to remind him he was a man. A man with needs.

His needs sure picked a hell of a time to make themselves known. Nick shifted uncomfortably in his jeans. Faith Kincade had caused this response the minute he'd laid eyes on her. She was the last woman in the world his libido needed to be interested in.

The woman was pregnant with Steve's child. Steve was dead. His brother had been married to Faith's sister. Hell, there wasn't a soap opera on television that could compare to this real-life mess. The mess that was his life. And Faith's. Those thoughts were better than a cold shower on his less than noble ideas concerning her.

Running fingers through his hair, Nick silently mocked himself. The last thing he'd let himself do was get caught in the deceitful woman's web. Not like Steve. *I'd better get a grip.* He wouldn't touch her if his life depended on it.

The thought offered no relief.

Faith struggled against the weight pressing down on her. It completely enveloped her and encased her limbs. Panic set in and she thrashed around—desperate to be free. Escape seemed impossible. She opened her eyes, but they didn't work.

Why can't I see? What is this place?

She finally managed to release her upper body and sit upright. The room was dark, but shadows emerged. A small cry slipped through her lips as next to her, a dark form took shape.

Scratching sounded as a match blazed to life. The tangy odor of sulfur seared her nostrils. The match touched the wick of a candle and was extinguished. Faith was wide-awake.

No, she had to be trapped in a nightmare. What other explanation was there for Nick Harrison to be towering over her as she lay in bed? What kind of hell had she stumbled into?

Soft, keening sounds rose from her throat. She pressed her back against the headboard when Nick reached toward her. His warm hand touched her shoulder—its heat scorched her through the material of her gown. How did she get into her gown?

"Faith." Nick's firm voice shattered the surreal mood pervading the room.

"You're…real?" She tried to understand what was happening. "It was the quilt. I couldn't get free from it…thought I was dead. Buried with Carrie and Steve."

At the mention of Steve's name, Nick pulled his hand back to his side. The chill of his shuttered expression replaced the warmth of his touch and she shivered.

Faith gathered her thoughts. She remembered the drive, but little else. Looking down to hide her confusion, she picked imaginary lint from her gown. *My gown. How did I get into my gown?* Startled, her gaze flew to Nick's face. Faith could feel the heat staining her cheeks.

Nick's lips quirked upward as though he knew what was going through her mind. He opened his mouth to speak.

Shuffling footsteps in the doorway drew their attention. Whatever explanation Nick might have offered never came.

Faith peered beyond him to see who had arrived. A tousle-haired woman stood in the doorway and lifted a lantern to illuminate the room.

Was Nick married?

"Looks like the storm knocked the electric out." The woman stepped closer to the bed. "How's the patient?"

Nick moved aside so Faith had an unobstructed view of the visitor. Light curls softened the woman's face and her gentle voice soothed Faith's agitation.

The woman stuck her hand out. "Name's Mab, not short for Mabel. Just, Mab." She shot Nick a mild glare. "You forget how to introduce people, cowboy?" Mab didn't seem to expect a reply. She set the lantern on the nightstand and perched herself on the edge of the bed. "Glad to see you're awake. You gave us quite a scare, can't remember seeing Nick in a situation he couldn't handle before." Mab grinned at Nick and he smiled back.

Faith almost envied their easy camaraderie.

"Nick called me over when you…arrived. I'm a nurse."

Faith offered a small smile and returned Mab's firm handshake. "I'm Faith Kincade, I guess Nick probably told you. I'm sorry you had to come out in such foul weather."

"It's just a quick jog through the trees. Wayne, my husband, is Nick's foreman so we live on the ranch."

At the mention of Nick's name, Faith glanced around the room. He was gone. She hadn't heard him leave. Instead of relief she felt…empty? *Must be a reaction to the fall.*

Turning her attention back to Mab, Faith hesitated to ask her next question. She had to know. Apprehension pushed the words past her tight throat.

"I…I fell pretty hard…I hit my head and side." She swallowed the knot that tried to block her power of speech. "The baby—"

"Is fine. As far as my examination went, you're showing no indications of miscarriage."

Faith squeezed her eyelids shut and offered a silent, heartfelt prayer of thanks. She opened her eyes when Mab lightly touched her arm.

"Any cramps or unusual twinges?"

"I don't think so. Some discomfort on my right side and my head aches."

"That'll be the bruises where you had a come-to-Jesus meeting with the gate and driveway. Flat on the ground." Mab patted her hand in a reassuring gesture. "Sorry to say they'll give you fits for a couple of days. Not to mention, they'll have more colors than the flag. Just let me know if anything changes. And don't let Nick tease you—I put you in your gown." Mab stood and rearranged the pillows and blankets.

Relief over the baby's condition left Faith feeling drained. All things considered, she'd come off lightly. Bruises she could live with, losing the baby she couldn't. She nestled deeper under the covers.

"Rest is the best thing for you and the baby." Mab paused. "Everything else will take care of itself…in time."

I hope so. Faith wished fervently.

Mab extinguished the candle and carried the lantern to the door. She stopped and called gently, "Night, Faith."

"Good night. Thank you so much." A yawn punctuated her answer. Faith slid down into the soft bedding. Sleep claimed her before the lantern's glow faded into the hallway.

Mab approached Nick as he lounged against the wall outside Faith's door. Judging by the expression on her face, he was in for it. *What the hell did I do now?*

"I like her." Mab paused, seeming to watch his face for a reaction. "Did you consider getting to know the woman before you condemned her?"

Nick raised an eyebrow. "The evidence is clear. She hasn't denied anything."

"Why would she? You really think she owes you any explanations?" Mab turned toward the stairs. "Harrison pride—I'll never understand it." Mumbling under her breath, she shuffled up the stairs to the guestroom.

Nick stared into the darkness long after she'd gone. Even after Mab's reassurances about Faith and the baby's condition he felt unsettled. Sleep would never come with his mind churned inside out. He turned and entered Faith's room.

Settling into the old wing chair, he stared in the direction of her soft breathing—reassured by the deep, smooth rhythm.

He'd have to be firm—no way would she worm her way under his skin.

A pair of wide eyes might fool Mab, but not me.

Quiet. A serene and peaceful quiet. The utter absence of traffic and regular morning sounds Faith was accustomed to pulled her kindly awake.

She stretched her arms above her head like a contented kitten. The twinge in her side made her pause midstretch and reminded her this was not a pleasure trip. And definitely not a relaxing vacation. It boiled down to a battle for Steve and Carrie's unborn child—her child.

The whinny of a horse cut through her gloomy thoughts. It was going to be a shame to replace such tranquil sounds with the noise of discord.

A realistic solution was available. Faith simply had to find it. *Simple, huh.* Keeping the baby was the only outcome she'd accept. She'd sell the bookstore and her house, if necessary, because losing the baby was not an option.

How was she going to accomplish that without revealing how the child had been conceived? Unconventional or not, it was still miraculous.

One day at a time—one hour at a time. That's how she'd get through whatever ordeals lay ahead.

Pushing the covers back, she noticed her surroundings for the first time. The burnished wood of the antique, four-post bed gleamed in the early-morning light. Flowered fabric hung at the windows and adorned the quilt on the bed. Although the room had seen a woman's touch at one time, the fabrics were now faded and worn.

Faith peeked into the adjoining bathroom. This was obviously the master suite. Why was she using it? Not that it mattered—hopefully she wouldn't have to stay long enough to figure it out. It was too much to worry about and right now all she wanted to think about was a shower—a long, hot shower.

Twenty minutes later, Faith emerged, refreshed and energized. Deciding to forego drying her hair to save time, she pinned it up off her neck. She left the hem of her shirt hanging out to conceal the front panel of her maternity jeans.

Faith walked to the dresser. The beveled mirror above it reflected her profile. She molded her hands over the small mound beneath her shirt that became more evident each day. The scope of what lay ahead seemed overwhelming.

"I won't let you down," she whispered to the baby. And to herself.

Following the mouthwatering aromas drifting in the air, she found herself outside the kitchen. The clatter of dishes and amiable murmur of voices covered her approach. Tinkling laughter stopped Faith before she pushed against the swinging door. A child?

Did Nick have a child? Was he married? Faith hadn't given much thought to those possibilities. Steve hadn't discussed his family and she realized just how scant her knowledge of the Harrison family was. But maybe it was for the best. She wasn't here to get close—only to find a way to leave.

Stepping into the room, Faith absorbed the domesticity of the scene playing before her and was content to remain in the background.

A large, round, table was the focal point of the room. The walls lined with knotty pine cupboards. Faith turned toward the one man who drew her attention.

Nick stood with his back toward her. Broad shoulders strained against the flannel shirt that confined them. Snug denim molded his muscular thighs.

Pancakes performed acrobatic flips from the spatula gripped in his hand, much to the delight of the laughing child perched on the counter near him. The child couldn't be older than four or five. Her giggles and clapping pulled a smile from Faith. Reaching out with his empty hand, Nick ruffled the girl's golden curls. Green eyes filled with adoration grinned up at him. Father and child?

Faith relaxed and rested her shoulder against the doorjamb. She turned her attention to the other people in the room.

Mab sat at the table. *Ah, ha.* It was easy to see where the child inherited her hair, Mab's curls hung past her shoulders in the same ringlets. A bear of a man straddled the chair next to the smiling woman. He slid his arm across the back of her chair and whispered into her ear. Whatever he said brought a rosy blush and smile to Mab's face. He had to be her husband, Wayne.

"Emily," Mab's soft voice drew the child's gaze, "how about sharing some of the attention you're giving Uncle Nick? Let him finish those pancakes or we won't eat until lunchtime."

Using a chair pulled next to the counter, Emily nimbly bounded to the floor. Her curious gaze settled on Faith.

"Hi." The child chirped a greeting and skipped toward her.

Faith straightened as all eyes focused on her. Nick glanced over his shoulder. The man who'd entertained a child was gone and in his place was the Nick Harrison she'd come to expect. Remote, cold, and full of condemnation. He turned back to the stove without uttering a word. She'd expected nothing less, but it still embarrassed her.

She swallowed the flicker of hurt his intentional snub caused as a small hand slipped into hers.

"I'm Emily. Daddy calls me Em." Shyness didn't appear to be an issue for the child.

Crouching down, she placed herself at Emily's level. "Good morning, Emily. My name's Faith. I'm glad to meet you."

The child returned her handshake. "Do you live here with Uncle Nick now?"

Nick swung around, and watched to see how she'd handle the question.

"Well...actually...I guess you could say I'm a...guest."

Faith heard Nick's derisive snort. She glanced uncertainly at Mab, who smiled encouragingly. "Maybe you could take me out later and introduce me to the horse I heard this morning— if it's okay with your mom and dad."

Covering her mouth, Emily erupted into a fit of giggles. "Silly, Uncle Nick has 'bout a bazillion horses. I only know just a little bit of them."

Faith laughed with her. "I suppose that would be silly to try and meet a 'bazillion' horses." The child was delightful. Pushing up, Faith's gasp ended the giggle session with Emily.

"Sore?" Mab's voice was filled with concern.

"I'm sporting all the colors of the rainbow this morning, stiff, too." Gingerly lowering herself into a chair, she ignored Nick's intense stare and tested the bump on her forehead with her fingertips.

Mab broke the silence. "Where are my manners? I'm getting to be as bad as Nick." She shot him a peevish look. "Faith, I'd like you to meet my husband. Wayne, this is Faith Kincade."

Wayne stood and tipped his hat. "Howdy. Em and I ducked over this morning to see how you were making out."

Faith was touched by his concern. "Thanks to Mab and Mr. Harrison, I'm in pretty good shape."

A plate clattered onto the table near her elbow and Faith flinched. Pleasantries were over.

Wayne lowered himself onto his seat.

A stack of fresh pancakes was heaped on the plate Nick placed next to her. She realized how hungry she was. Yesterday's lunch seemed a lifetime ago.

"Thank you." Faith's gaze followed Nick around the table.

He chose a chair as far from her as possible in the cozy kitchen. He didn't bother to acknowledge she'd spoken.

The icy coldness of his stare curbed her appetite. Knowing the baby relied on her to stay healthy, she managed to choke down the first bite. It went down like sand and lay in her stomach, heavy as a rock.

Mab sent a sidelong look at Wayne. Nick's rudeness seemed to be making them all uncomfortable.

Wayne broke the strained silence. "I'm about finished here." He prodded Nick with his elbow. "Let's head out and check those fresh foals."

Nick grunted.

Faith stabbed another bite of pancake with her fork. *Gee, a caveman sound to go with his Neanderthal tendencies.*

Scraping his chair back, Nick stood and nodded at Mab. Tapping a finger on the tip of Emily's nose, he followed Wayne out the back door.

Seething, Faith focused on her plate. Heaven knew she hadn't expected things to be easy, but the open hostility Nick had shown in front of Mab and the others dismayed her. It was humiliating. As if she ought to feel ashamed. *That'll be a cold day in hell.*

Cordiality and plain good manners were evidently not going to be a part of this setup. Nick had set the rules of engagement and it wasn't going to be pretty.

A bite at a time, she managed to finish her breakfast. Mab sipped coffee and allowed her time to gather herself together. Emily moved down onto the pine floor, dumped a bucket of plastic farm animals, and was absorbed immediately in make-believe.

After Faith drained the final swallow of milk from her glass, Mab set her own cup down. Time to face another hurdle. It seemed to be what her days were reduced to. She waited for the woman, who'd been so kind to her, to speak.

Mab didn't keep her waiting. "Give him time."

Faith didn't need to ask who the "him" was.

"Steve's death hit hard." Mab paused and shook her head. "Learning about the baby has been a shock for him."

She wanted to ease Mab's discomfort. "This hasn't been easy for anyone. People deal with things in their own ways—in their own time."

Mab nodded as they reached for the breakfast dishes at the same time. Exchanging grins, they finished clearing the table together. Then Mab filled the sink with soapy water and Faith grabbed a towel to dry with.

Looking around to ensure that Emily was still busy with her make-believe world, Mab spoke softly while they worked. "Things started to fall apart for the Harrison family about twenty years ago." She passed a dripping plate to Faith. "Long before Wayne or I came."

Intrigued, Faith continued drying and stacking the dishes Mab passed to her. She'd wondered what caused the estrangement between Steve and his family. Curiosity won out over good sense.

"My room looks like a master suite." Faith hesitated, reluctant to pry, but felt compelled to discover more about the family her baby would be born into. "Why am I using it?"

The silence stretched so long, she feared she'd overstepped her boundaries. Faith opened her mouth to apologize, but Mab spoke first.

"I expect you'll hear it from busybody townsfolk eventually." Mab's hands rested in the limp suds—a faraway look on her face.

"If you're uncomfortable talking about it, just tell me to mind my own business." Faith lay a hand on her belly. "I don't want you to feel like a gossip."

Mab glanced at the spot where Faith's hand rested. Determination came into her eyes. "No, it's your family now." She continued to wash the dishes. "About twenty years ago, Nick's mother ran off with another man."

Faith stared at Mab. *My God, no wonder Steve never mentioned his mother.* "What about her children?"

"She never looked back. Never contacted them or her husband. It shattered the three boys."

Faith froze. She must have misunderstood. "Three boys? I thought it was just Nick and Steve."

"No, there were three. Nick, Steve and Logan—the youngest."

Faith shook her head in disbelief. Steve had been reluctant to discuss his family, but this was deplorable. *Talk about dysfunctional.*

When the last dish was dried, Mab motioned Faith to a chair. "Let's get you sitting if we're going to chat. That hip has to be aching."

Faith nodded.

Mab topped off her cup of coffee before sitting. "Steve never mentioned Logan?"

"Steve didn't mention his family. Period. Carrie and I eventually stopped asking." Why hadn't they pushed him for information?

"Carrie?"

"My sister—Steve's wife." Faith gripped her hands together on top of the table. How much did the kind woman know of Nick's twist on the baby? "Mab, what, exactly, has Nick told you about this…situation?"

Mab averted her gaze, staring into the coffee cup.

"Don't worry about offending me. I'd like to know where I stand." She leaned forward hoping to encourage an honest answer.

"Nick returned from the lawyer's office mighty put out. It took Wayne a couple of days to get him to talk about it."

Faith nodded. It seemed logical so far.

"All he'd tell Wayne was that Steve left his share of the ranch to his baby," Mab continued. "His unborn baby. And that Steve's sister-in-law was pregnant with the child."

Faith was thankful to see only curiosity in Mab's eyes, not the disgust she'd thought the news would elicit. "Hearing it put that way, I'm surprised he didn't leave me out in the rain last night."

"It'd never happen." Mab's tone sounded confidant. "Mr. Harrison ruled those boys, taught them good manners—if nothing else." Her lips thinned into a tight line.

"Where is Mr. Harrison?" Faith couldn't help but ask.

"Passed on almost a year ago. Too young." She brushed crumbs from the table and tossed them into the sink. "He never recovered from his wife's betrayal. Neither did the boys, for that matter.''

''What do you mean?''

''Soon as Steve was able, he took off for college. Sent a postcard when the mood hit him. Nick hadn't heard from him in nearly eighteen months when he heard about the accident.''

''Didn't Nick know where to find him?'' Faith felt a weight settle in her gut.

''No. For the first few years, Nick spent his own money on private detectives, just so he'd know where Steve was. He finally decided it was his brother's choice to stay distant.''

Faith trembled. What if Nick hadn't known? All of her assumptions about him might be based on nothing more than empty air. She'd assumed he had known about Steve and Carrie's marriage. Had ignored them, purposely. Did it matter?

Faith forced herself to set speculation aside and learn the rest. ''What about the youngest—Logan?''

''Left the ranch about seven months after Steve. I'm afraid old Mr. Harrison cultivated a lot of resentment in those boys. Nick only heard from Logan once, and that was over two years ago.'' She shook her head. ''He put a detective on his trail after Steve died.''

Faith could not fathom a family so deeply shattered. So far separated from one another.

Mab shook her head. ''Haven't been able to let him know about his father or Steve.''

''Or, that he'll be an uncle.'' A film of moisture blurred Faith's vision and she blinked rapidly. ''He probably won't be any more thrilled than Nick.'' She looked into Mab's kind eyes. ''Things aren't always…well…what they appear.''

Eyes full of confusion, Mab stared at her. Faith wanted so badly to confide and share the truth about the baby. The slamming of the back door caused them both to jump.

''Uncle Nick!'' Emily abandoned her game and ran headlong at the man. His muscled arms swung her up and he kissed the top of her head. She squealed in delight and he put her back down.

How long had Nick been standing outside the door? How much had he overheard? Faith frantically searched her memory for what she and Mab had discussed. Angry with herself for feeling like an errant schoolgirl, she stood.

"Thanks again for last night, Mab." Faith ignored Nick and headed out of the room. She almost made it.

"Miss Kincade." Nick's voice stopped her before she made it through the door.

Squaring her shoulders, Faith turned to face him. "Yes, Mr. Harrison." She refused to allow him to intimidate her.

"You're interested in Harrison family history?"

Her cheeks burned with annoyance.

Emily glanced back and forth between them. She seemed confused by Nick's tone.

Curbing her initial urge to verbally attack the man, Faith kept her voice even so she wouldn't alarm the child. "I'm interested in anything that might affect my baby."

Mab lifted Emily onto her hip and murmured a hasty goodbye. She slipped out the back door.

Smart lady, keep Emily out of the crossfire.

Circling past Faith, Nick scrubbed his hands at the sink.

That's it, ignore me.

He dried his hands on the towel she'd used earlier. "Thought you'd like to see the ranch—get to know the place."

Suspicion clouded her mind. She must have misunderstood. "Excuse me?" She tried not to stare at his strong fingers when he tossed the towel onto the counter.

Nick stepped to within a foot of where she stood and studied her face. Faith could feel the heat from his body surrounding her. She resisted the urge to back away.

Nick's calm voice continued. "Aren't you interested in the ranch?" His eyes glittered. "The place where the baby will be raised."

Faith's bewilderment must have been written on her face.

Nick's lips curved into a thin smile, devoid of humor. "When I'm awarded custody, Miss Kincade."

Faith's stunned expression almost caused Nick to regret his blunt words. But he didn't believe in anything less than the truth. Harsh as it seemed, he wanted his cards out in the open.

He'd done that all right.

He wanted to leave no doubt in her mind where they stood. The baby was a Harrison and it belonged on the Whispering Moon as surely as he did. Nick was determined to do whatever it took to ensure the outcome.

Too many Harrisons left and never returned. The unborn child stayed. Nick resolved to see this through, no matter the emotional cost to himself—or Faith.

CHAPTER FOUR

SO MUCH for the fine art of subtlety. Nick had taken it down to the bare knuckles. If he expected Faith to wilt like some helpless Victorian miss, he had much to learn about the Kincade stubbornness.

"I'll just grab a jacket and boots." Faith headed down the hall, turned to face him before disappearing from view. "My child is bound to be curious about the ranch when it's older, I'll want to be able to describe it in great detail. It will make him feel as though he'd seen it himself."

Flashing a brilliant smile, she stepped out of sight on legs that threatened to leave her flat on the floor. Her show of bravado was an illusion, but he didn't need to know. She'd seen the vein pounding at his temple. Heaven help her if he called her bluff.

Retrieving her things, she hurried back. Nick glared out the window above the sink with both of his hands gripping the basin. She hoped he wasn't imagining it was her neck. Absorbed in his own thoughts, he didn't seem aware of her presence.

Slipping gloves from her pockets, Faith pulled them over her trembling fingers. "I'm ready, Mr. Harrison."

Turning to face her, Nick's steely gaze took in her barn coat and rubber boots. "Let's go. I've wasted enough of my day."

Long strides ate up the ground. Faith jogged in an attempt to keep from falling behind. *I won't ask him to slow down.*

Scenery flowed by in a blur. Impressions passed before she could form a picture in her mind. Faith slowed when she felt the twinges of a stitch in her side, she wasn't about to risk the baby trying to match pace with Neanderthal man.

41

Thick grass cushioned her steps. Wildflowers bordered the white picket fence that enclosed the backyard. Bright splashes of color darted by as songbirds flocked to the feeders scattered about the area.

Following the well-worn path, Faith scanned ahead at the thick trees. Winded, she spoke up. "Mr. Harrison, please…" She stopped and took several deep breaths. "I can't keep up with you."

She hated to admit any weakness to him.

Nick turned and stomped to where she stood. His gaze was focused on her middle and she saw his jaw unclench. He motioned her to a nearby stump. "I'm not used to being around a, um…"

It was as close to an apology as she was likely to hear from him, so she committed it to memory. "I believe, pregnant woman is the term you need. It's not a dirty word." Faith glanced around, unable to meet his sardonic gaze. In his mind, her condition was the worst kind of dirt.

Swiveling around on her makeshift seat, she took in the natural serenity of her surroundings. Ponderosa Pines swayed in the breeze and aspen leaves danced. Visible farther up the path, she caught a glimpse of the barn. Its boards weathered to a soft gray patina by the elements.

Closing her eyes, Faith emptied her mind and simply enjoyed existing. A playful breeze tossed strands of hair across her face and tickled her cheek. Smiling, she brushed the errant locks aside. When she opened her eyes, Nick was staring at her.

Self-conscious, she lowered her head and brushed imaginary dust from her jeans to avoid his penetrating gaze. Faith could feel the heat that glowed in her cheeks. He enjoyed making her squirm, why else would he stare so intently?

Standing, she walked back to the path. "I'll try to do a better job of keeping up."

Nick didn't respond, but Faith noticed he shortened his stride.

The old barn was a wonder. According to Nick, it was

over sixty years old and hand-built by his grandfather. Pride resonated in his voice every time he mentioned the ranch. Faith felt generations of care seeping from the wooden structure as they entered.

Somehow, the smell of horses, hay and dust combined into a comforting haze. Faith counted eight stalls easily accommodated by the cavernous expanse. The tack room door stood ajar and she wandered inside.

Preoccupied with exploring the nooks and crannies hidden away, Faith forgot to think of Nick as the enemy. For this moment in time, he was her tour guide. She leaned close to a nearby saddle and inhaled deeply.

"Mmm...nothing like the smell of leather." Faith removed a glove and ran her palm across the well-worn seat. "Looks like this one gets some use."

"It's mine."

Nick's words propelled her hand from the saddle faster than if a rattler coiled there. Images of the part of his anatomy used to soften the leather of the seat rose unbidden in her mind. The butter-soft leather would mold to his muscles.

Raging, out-of-control hormones were certainly to blame for her wayward thoughts. *This is Nick Harrison.* She scolded herself harshly. Fantasizing about his posterior didn't necessarily mean she was a sex fiend. However, it did make her a certifiable idiot.

Strolling ahead of him so he wouldn't see the heat in her face, Faith forced her attention on the surroundings. Thank heavens he wasn't a mind reader. She risked a glance at him. The smug grin on his face made her wish she hadn't.

Stopping in front of the nearest stall, Faith looked in and fell crazy in love with the two magnificent creatures staring back at her. Standing protectively in front of a newborn foal, a gold colored mare watched her warily.

Faith rested her arms on top of the stall's half-door. She spoke in a hushed tone to the mare and tried to coax her close enough to touch.

"Try these." Nick slipped two sugar cubes into her hand. "Lady has a wicked sweet tooth."

Wicked was exactly the right word for the turn Faith's thoughts took. The brush of Nick's fingers on the sensitive skin of her palm sent a flow of liquid fire racing up her arm.

Turning away from his curious gaze, Faith clicked her tongue. Lady nickered and came over to investigate the displayed cubes. Gingerly her velvet muzzle nudged Faith's outstretched hand and Lady consumed the treat with a dainty touch. Faith sighed, entranced.

"I can see why you call her Lady. She has perfect manners." Faith patted Lady's neck when the mare gave her shoulder a nudge.

Lady returned to the foal and gave it a gentle push with her nose.

Tipping her head back, Faith smiled at Nick. "Butterscotch, that's the perfect word for their coloring. What kind of horse are they? How old is the baby?" Excitement caused her to momentarily forget to keep her distance.

Nick watched the horses for long seconds. "Lady here is one of our best brood mares. The ranch is earning a reputation for producing show-quality Palominos." He jerked his head toward the foal. "Lady's new one is two days old."

"But he seems so steady."

"*She* stood within minutes. Foals usually do." Nick opened a nearby barrel and scooped some grain.

Faith watched him pour the mixture into the feed bucket inside the stall. She'd seen horses before, but never so close. Especially a newborn foal. The foal stepped closer to investigate Faith and she brushed gentle strokes on its satiny nose.

"What's her name?"

"No name yet." Nick rested his backside against the stall door.

"What a shame. Every baby deserves a name."

Looking toward him, the grim set of his mouth made her realize how she sounded. Faith kicked the toe of her boot into the sawdust covering the floor of the barn. She felt the pleasure of the past thirty minutes evaporate like steam from a kettle. Everything came back to the baby she carried.

"Name her." He spoke without looking at her.

Faith looked up sharply, certain she'd misunderstood his words. "What?"

"Pick a name. Mab and Emily have named dozens. They won't begrudge you one."

Too startled by the offer to voice an objection, Faith didn't bother to hide her pleasure. Watching the foal's antics for a few more minutes, she decided.

"Toffee." Faith ran her fingers through the vanilla-gold mane of the filly. She met its wide-eyed gaze. "She's sweet natured and toffee colored."

Nick's lips curved into an easy smile. The harsh expression Faith was accustomed to seeing melted from his features. A dimple was chiseled into his cheek, new to her simply because his smile had never been turned in her direction. She tamped down the heat such a small detail started deep inside her.

"We'd best get moving if you want to see the rest before lunch." Nick started toward the far end of the barn. His mouth a taut line, as though he regretted lowering his defenses. The line of his spine rigid.

Faith offered the foal one more pat. "Bye, Toffee."

Nick waited outside, a scowl had replaced his smile and he didn't meet her eyes. Stepping next to him, Faith faced a newer building. This was not a simple one-barn operation. No wonder he'd thought she was after the ranch—it was obviously worth a great deal of money. And he'd invested his whole life in it.

"Exactly how big is the Whispering Moon?"

"Twenty-five hundred acres, more or less." Nick's saddle-brown eyes glowed while he talked. "We use the original barn for the brood mares and foals. The new facility houses the indoor arena and stalls for two dozen more horses."

"Who's we?"

"Wayne and I. He's been here for sixteen years. Came

here as foreman when I was eighteen. Most of what I know about horses he had to beat into my thick skull.'' He continued toward the second barn.

Faith passed through the doors behind him. Her attention was drawn to the sound of voices at the far side of the indoor arena.

''It looks like our trainer's here.'' Nick headed to where Wayne talked with another man. ''Have a look around, I have to take care of some business.''

Watching as Nick approached the two men, she noticed that he stood a head taller than either man. Snatches of conversation began to drift toward her. Not wanting to be nosy, Faith turned to look at the rest of the facility.

Peeking into the stalls and multiple rooms occupied only a few minutes. Noticing that the men were still engrossed in conversation, she slipped out a side door into the late-morning sunshine. After the emotional swells of the past half hour, she needed a break from Nick's disconcerting presence.

A dog barked nearby and drew her attention to a cozy, white clapboard house set in the pines. Emily tore around the corner of the house and tossed a ball to a small terrier that scampered to retrieve it. Bounding back with the prize clamped in his teeth, the dog accepted Emily's lavish hugs.

Faith trotted toward them. A smile pulled at her lips. She'd stumbled upon the Lee family home, just what she needed to distract her from the confusing feelings Nick provoked in her.

Emily glanced up. Squealing, she ran to Faith. ''Miss Faith, you found us.'' The child grabbed her hand. ''Want some cookies? Mama just made 'em.''

''If you're sure she won't mind if we snitch a few.''

''Oh, no, 'specially if *you* ask. 'Cuz you're growed up.''

Faith couldn't refuse the imploring gaze focused on her. *Smart kid, Mab probably told her no ten times already.*

Passing the exhausted dog, Faith leaned down to ruffle the fur on the top of his head. He licked her fingers and settled down to snooze in the sun.

She pressed a hand to the small of her back as she straightened. Her growing belly was making itself felt. "Looks like you wore him out."

"Buster plays and sleeps. Oh, sometimes he eats, too." Emily stared up at her. "Miss Faith?"

"Hmm?"

"Why's your tummy so big?"

Surprised by the question, she gathered her thoughts before answering. "Because I have a baby growing there. Just like you grew in your mama's tummy."

Emily scrunched her face in concentration. "Does it have a daddy, too?"

Such an innocent question to thrust so deeply into Faith's heart. Luckily Emily lost interest before Faith had to come up with an answer. Pulled along, Faith found herself at the front door.

Mab stood inside the screen door, wiping her hands on her gingham apron. Pushing the door open, she offered Faith a bright smile. "Hope she didn't talk your ear off. She tends to be curious."

"Heavens, no. We've had a wonderful chat. Is this a bad time?" Faith rambled.

"Are you kidding? You're just the opportunity Emily's been praying for." Mab led the way inside with a laugh. "Having a guest means her chances of eating a cookie before lunch are increased."

Faith took in the surroundings as they passed through the house. It suited Mab. Open and bright. A delightful mixture of old and new.

"Your home is lovely."

"Thank you. I think after twelve years it's beginning to feel complete."

"You weren't married when Wayne came to the ranch?" She followed Mab into the homey kitchen. The aroma of fresh-baked cookies set her mouth watering.

Mab motioned her into a chair. Oven mitts in place, she checked the current batch of cookies in the oven. Emily settled herself across the table from Faith and helped herself to a cookie.

Mab turned to Faith. "Wayne was here about four years before we met. He came into the emergency room where I was on duty. Arm busted in two places." She shook her head. "Fool tried to break every bone in his body. Fell out of the hayloft in the old barn. How could I resist?"

Faith smiled. Some people were destined to find each other.

Mab carried a pitcher of milk to the table and the three of them munched on cookies. Faith took another bite and knew she'd found heaven. She asked a question that had festered since her talk with Mab had been interrupted. "Were Steve and Logan still here when you came?"

"Not for long. Things ran differently around here while the elder Mr. Harrison was alive."

Faith could see by the deep frown on Mab's face that it hadn't been a good thing.

"The boys pretty much kept to themselves." Mab continued. "Except Nick. He and Wayne hit it off." She glanced sideways and seemed to notice Emily's attention focused on her and changed the subject. "Then we were blessed with Emily. We had just about given up on ever having a child. Amazing the difference a baby makes."

Evidently realizing she'd wandered onto shaky ground, Mab stood and pulled the last pan of cookies from the oven.

"Mama, Miss Faith has a baby in her tummy." Emily barged in where conversational angels feared to tread. "Will it make a difference, too?"

Faith met Mab's eyes across the room. She answered for the flustered mother. "Yes, honey. This baby makes all the difference in the world."

Faith hurried back to the main house to prepare the evening meal. Mab had tried to talk her out of it before she'd left, saying it was something she normally took care of. But Faith had insisted. Nick welcomed her about as much as a burr under his saddle, but she wasn't a freeloader. She'd pull her own weight.

He doesn't need to know I love cooking.

Organizing the needed ingredients, Faith rolled up her sleeves and lost herself in the preparations. Twenty minutes later, she placed the pan in the oven. A glance at her watch confirmed there was plenty of time to freshen up before the men came looking for a hot meal.

She pushed the door to her room open. Three boxes were stacked in the center of the floor where someone had carried them in from the trunk of her car. The bookcase in the corner stood empty of its previous clutter.

She pulled her favorite pictures and books from the boxes. It was time to put her mark on the room. Even though the length of her stay was uncertain, she still needed to feel that one place in the house was hers.

Emptying two of the boxes, she folded them flat and slid them under the bed. She decided that the third box would have to wait until after dinner and pushed it into the closet.

Satisfied with the changes she'd wrought, Faith hurried to wash up. Cold water splashed on her face refreshed her and helped her feel more prepared to face another meeting with Nick.

The man was a study in contrasts. One moment he acted like the villain and the next he let her name a foal. Faith couldn't get a handle on which was the real Nick Harrison. Maybe he was an amalgamation of both.

It was too much to analyze she thought as she headed to the dining room. Having prepared the table earlier, plates and silver gleamed under the bright overhead light. Uncertain of the regular dinner routine, Faith acted on instinct, and hunted around for napkins.

The phone rang in the kitchen. Faith headed toward the swinging door and placed her hand against the solid wood, but stopped when the sound of heavy footsteps hurried through the kitchen.

Nick's voice interrupted the ringing. "Nick Harrison here."

She turned from the door to give him some privacy.

"Do you have the report on Kincade yet?" His words knifed through her.

Faith felt her blood drain toward her feet. Shamelessly she edged closer to the door that divided the rooms. The silence stretched and tension crawled up her spine, causing her scalp to tingle.

"Nothing? Look, you're my attorney. Find me something we can take to court."

Faith's fingernails cut into her palms.

"No one is squeaky clean. I can't petition the court for custody without something concrete to back it up."

Fury grew then, boiling inside Faith. How dare he have her investigated? But why was she surprised? Nick had warned her he'd do whatever was necessary to take the baby from her. This was her wake-up call. Obviously she couldn't let her guard down.

"I know. Yes, I understand." Nick's tone was harsh. Whatever his attorney said wasn't what he wanted to hear. "Why are her medical files sealed?"

She squeezed her eyes closed and took deep breaths to keep from jumping on Nick's back and scratching his eyes out. Knocking him upside the head with a large stick would make Faith feel better, but it wouldn't change the facts. Nick Harrison had appointed himself judge and jury. Judged and sentenced by him, she had no choice but to come out swinging. Wouldn't that look good before the judge? Psychotic woman attacks her baby's uncle.

"Can the records be obtained with a subpoena?"

It just kept getting worse. Faith gripped the doorjamb when her knees threatened to buckle. Complete confidentiality had been guaranteed by the clinic. They had to abide by that agreement, didn't they?

Ramming the door with both hands, Faith prepared to confront Nick. Water running into the sink prevented him from hearing her approach. He cradled the phone between his ear and shoulder while he scrubbed his hands.

"What about her neighbors? Friends? Anyone she confided in?" He rinsed his hands and reached, blindly, for the towel. "Call me when—" Nick's words cut off as Faith shoved a towel into his hand.

She'd caught him off guard and his surprise showed, but he recovered quickly. Solemn, his gaze locked with hers as he finished his conversation under her hostile stare.

"Do what you can. Explore any options we can use." Lowering the receiver onto the base, Nick casually folded his arms.

As though he hadn't just cut out her heart and ground it under his heel.

"What right do you have to pry into my life?" Faith's agitation built with each word. "Who do you think you are?"

"The man who's going to get custody of that baby. I gave you fair warning." His calm words provoked her further. "Whatever's necessary, remember?"

"What is it about me that bothers you? You don't know me."

"I know your kind."

"My *kind?*" Faith was astounded. What kind of backward mentality lurked behind his handsome face?

Nick casually strode to look out the window, then walked back to face her. "Come on, Miss Kincade. You stand there lecturing me from your soapbox and in your belly is the baby that should have been your sister's." His eyes narrowed. "That's the *kind* I'm talking about."

His barbs wounded Faith deeply, but not for the reasons he believed. Something Mab mentioned earlier slid into place.

"Do you judge every woman by the standard your mother set?"

Her soft words seemed to strike Nick square in the middle of his forehead. Before he had time to recover from her first strike, she pressed the advantage. "Judge me for who I am, not who you believe me to be.'' Rubbing her arms, Faith turned her gaze to the window. "Everyone has reasons for the decisions they make. Maybe you should accept this child for the miracle it is, for you, as well as me.''

He put his warm hand on her arm. "Tell me your reasons.'' His words were a persuasive whisper. "Give me a reason to trust this *miracle*.''

Faith wanted, no, needed to share her burden with someone. Longing welled within her. But, thankfully, reality returned before she opened her mouth.

Before her stood the one person in the world she couldn't confide in. Not yet. The hand resting on her arm might be kind, the eyes imploring, threatening to crumble her defenses. But Nick Harrison had the power to whisk her dreams and her future, from her arms.

Faith eased her arm from Nick's enticing touch. She stepped out of reach, unable to take such an irrevocable step. Anything she might reveal today could be used against her in a court battle—too much was on the line.

Mistrust, and a fleeting shadow that could have been disappointment, replaced the enigmatic look in Nick's eyes.

She'd made the only decision possible, so why did it feel so wrong? Why did it leave her feeling more alone?

Tension pulsated between them, thickening the air. Faith felt the tenuous thread they'd formed disintegrate. They were back to square one. She'd been a fool to imagine they could come to an unconstrained solution. The veins in Nick's neck stood out as though he only barely controlled his anger.

They both jumped when the back door flew open and bounced off the wall behind it. Emily bounded into the room—a bundle of pure energy that launched itself at Nick's chest as he scooped the laughing child into the air. His gaze locked with Faith's and he spoke without saying a word. This was only a reprieve. The next round wasn't far off.

Mab and Wayne strolled into the kitchen, hand-in-hand. The sight of Nick tickling Emily with his rough, day-old whiskers caused Faith's stomach to clench. She had to turn away to banish the image of his roughened chin scraping the sensitive skin of her own throat.

I'm going out of my ever-loving mind.

"Hope we're not too early." Mab moved to stand next to Faith. "There was no way to keep Emily away any longer. Anything I can help with?"

Faith pasted a bright smile on her lips. No way was she going to pull the Lee family into the problems between her and Nick. "That'd be great. I'm still trying to locate the cloth napkins."

Mab headed to the dining room. She kept talking over her shoulder. "Now don't go spoiling these cowboys or they'll expect dinner in the dining room every night."

"I wasn't sure what the norm was…" Faith followed her out of the kitchen.

"Don't go fretting. I'm just teasing." Mab whipped the napkins from the back of a drawer. "When's your next visit to the doctor?"

"I'll be seeing an obstetrician in Colorado Springs soon. He was recommended by my doctor. It beats driving three hours north every two weeks." Faith told her his name. Mab confirmed she'd heard only good things about the man.

Faith tried to ignore the curiosity in Mab's eyes.

Conversation around the table centered on the ranch. Faith listened intently, fascinated with the multifaceted operation. She'd no idea of the complexity in running such a facility.

Wayne and Mab did their best to include her. Nick ignored her.

Faith didn't have the emotional energy to dwell on the phone call she'd interrupted earlier. She relaxed and let the conversation flow around her. Emily chattered nonstop. Faith listened patiently and inserted the appropriate comments when necessary.

"There's a new baby horse, Miss Faith."

"You mean Lady's foal?"

"Uh-huh, wanna see after supper?" Emily chewed carefully, waiting for a reply.

"Actually, Nick was kind enough to show me around the barns this morning." Faith glanced up and found him staring at her. Flustered, she focused on Emily. "Toffee's a real beauty."

Emily tipped her head sideways and wrinkled her nose. "Toffee?"

A lull in the table conversation left all eyes focused on Faith. "The new foal. Nick let me name her." She watched as Mab looked at Nick. Wayne's eyebrows lifted.

Nick didn't see either reaction because he studied Faith with a hooded expression. Shifting in her chair, she wished he'd look at something else. Anything else. But, there was no escaping the intensity in his gaze.

Wayne settled back in his chair and patted his stomach.

"Faith, you're wasting a God given talent running a bookstore. We need to set you up in a diner."

"Watch out, Faith." Mab curved a hand over her husband's shoulder. "Once they find out you can cook, you end up chained to the stove."

Confused, Emily leaned close to Faith and whispered. "Don't worry, Miss Faith, I won't really let them do that."

Her stage whisper echoed in the quiet.

Wayne bellowed with laughter. Mab giggled. Faith checked Nick's reaction under her eyelashes. He coughed to cover his smile. It was amazing what his smile did to her equilibrium.

Captured by the merriment in his eyes, Faith's heart flipped over. Glimpses of a Nick Harrison she never would have believed existed kept throwing themselves at her.

She didn't like it, not at all. It was easier to deal with the man when he was merely the bad guy. Silently calling herself every kind of fool, she stood and stacked the dinner plates. The laughter tapered as Mab helped her clear the table.

Resisting an urge to glance toward the head of the table, Faith carried an armload of dishes to the kitchen. Placing them on the counter, she rested her aching forehead in her hand. She closed her eyes and mentally listed the reasons she disliked Nick. The reasons she didn't trust him. It was becoming more difficult to remember.

Damn him anyway. How dare he work his way under her skin. Hadn't she learned her lesson with Devon? The baby mattered. Nothing else.

Nick had hurt Carrie by refusing to acknowledge her marriage to Steve. Faith's conscience reared its meddling head. All right, so she couldn't be certain that Nick knew about the marriage. Mab said Steve hadn't kept in touch with his family, sometimes for years at a time.

It just didn't make sense. Conflicting emotions warred in her mind. What was her dislike of Nick based on? Even if he hadn't known about Carrie, he'd still given her the best reason a woman needed to dislike a man. Nick threatened her very reason for existing. Her baby.

The baby Carrie and Steve had been traveling to the Whispering Moon Ranch to tell him about. The trip that had ended their lives. It was a vicious circle, no beginning and no ending.

Faith wiped the back of her hand across her eyes to stem the tears that threatened to spill. She turned the water on to rinse the plates.

Mab's voice carried to her through the swinging door. "Hey, Faith, Emily voted for ice cream. How about we treat you to a cone in town?"

Flipping the tap off, she pushed the door to the dining room wide-open. Focusing on Emily she acted on instinct, instead of analyzing the options into a pulp. "If you're treating, I'm eating. Try and stop me." She grabbed Emily's hand and challenged the others. "Last one in the car does the dishes."

Faith savored the coolness on her tongue. The double-dip chocolate cone was a bit much, but it tasted heavenly sliding down her throat.

Squeezing into a corner booth at Nellie's Ice Cream Delight was difficult. They were shoulder to shoulder in the booth, but with the size of the crowd, they were lucky even to have seats. Wayne grumbled good-naturedly under his breath when Mab teased him about the dishes waiting when they returned to the ranch. It seemed washing dishes was not his idea of a good time.

"Well, Mr. Boy Scout. If you hadn't held the door for the womenfolk you wouldn't be in this fix." Mab laughed with no real sympathy in her voice.

Faith joined in her laughter. "If it's any consolation, Wayne, I appreciated the gesture." She tried once again to pull her leg away from where it touched Nick's hard thigh under the table.

In the scramble and confusion of sliding into the booth, Faith ended up sandwiched between the wall and Nick. Not exactly the situation she needed right now. It was unclear how he felt about their physical proximity, as his expression was unreadable.

Hemmed in by the wall meant no escape from the heat of his body. Her efforts to focus on the conversation were hindered by his cologne. Faith inhaled again. No, she was wrong. It was simply the smell of clean male skin. Nick's skin.

Girlfriend, you've finally gone over the edge. But what a way to go. Laura would slap her silly and Faith knew she deserved it. Stiffening her backbone, she felt in control of her adolescent hormones again.

For all of two seconds.

Nick leaned over and licked her ice-cream cone. Shock held her motionless as his hand covered hers while he spun the cone. The tip of his tongue circled the base where it was beginning to drip.

God help her, she'd never wanted to be an ice-cream cone so desperately.

This is Nick Harrison. This is Nick Harrison.

The silent mantra did nothing to cool the heat pooled in forbidden places. She nearly dumped the cone in her lap.

Maybe it'll put out the fire.

"It looked like you needed some help." Nick's deep voice broke through.

Faith licked her dry lips. "Help?" She croaked.

"With your ice cream."

"Ice cream?"

Nick looked at her through half-lowered lids. His half smile let her know he was aware of her reaction. Faith felt like an idiot. She glanced across the table, grateful that Mab and Wayne were too busy keeping Emily clean to witness her humiliation.

She risked another look at Nick. The banked fires deep in his eyes mesmerized her. Knowing he'd been affected, on some level, confused and frightened her. The last thing either of them needed was a physical attraction. But right now it was the only thing she desired.

"Oh!" She placed a hand on her stomach and waited for the baby to flutter again.

"What's wrong?"

Rather than answer, she reached for his hand. Pulling it toward her, she felt him tense. "It's okay."

Laying his large, warm hand against her stomach, she covered it with her own. The baby didn't keep them waiting for long before a well-aimed nudge from inside pushed at their hands. Nick's gaze flew to her face and she saw her own wonder and excitement mirrored in his eyes. Realizing the intimacy of the gesture, Faith removed her hand from his and looked away.

She cleared her throat before speaking in a tone only loud enough for Nick. "I thought you should be one of the first to feel it move. Thank you for sharing this." She felt heat climb up her neck and settle in her cheeks. "It makes it seem more real to share it."

He didn't answer. Faith flinched when she felt his hand settle more firmly on her middle. Out of view of the rest of the table, his hand molded itself to her belly—as though he had been touching her forever.

The next day passed with Nick making no reference to what they'd shared at the ice-cream parlor. Faith began to believe she'd imagined the whole thing.

Then, Nick would look at her. Just a look. Without saying a word he let her know he was thinking about those intimate moments, both the kicking baby and the touch of his tongue to her ice cream.

Time passed quickly while she made herself useful. Lawyers and custody battles weren't mentioned. It was an uncertain truce, but she grabbed at it with thankful hands so as not to shatter the tentative friendship they'd touched on.

Exploring the ranch house was interesting, but it filled her with a melancholy mood. Long ago the house offered shelter to loving couples and laughing children. It had protected a family. Faith wondered if Nick remembered any of the happy times before his mother had destroyed his trust and his family. And she wondered how a woman could walk away from her children?

The house offered no answers.

Smuggling carrots and sugar cubes to the horses, she was soothed and comforted by the time she spent with them. She was certain Nick knew of her spoiling of the animals, but like her, he seemed reluctant to destroy the congenial mood that had settled on the farmhouse.

Mab invited her for tea most afternoons. Emily's antics never failed to make Faith laugh. The lazy days of summer passed in a dreamlike haze of denial and desperate grasping for a sense of peace.

Her upcoming doctor appointment hadn't been mentioned since the night of the dinner party. She'd have forgotten it herself if it weren't for the note she'd taped to her bathroom mirror.

The day of the appointment dawned with a gentle rain tapping against the roof. They did need the rain, but she didn't relish driving in it. Excitement that even the rain couldn't squelch prodded her out of bed. Another ultrasound was scheduled for today. She'd see the baby.

Energized after a warm shower, she was determined to make today a special occasion. Faith slipped a silky pantsuit on and rummaged through her handbag until she located the directions to the office. Something was missing from her purse.

Where are my keys?

Spilling the contents of her purse onto the bed confirmed the absence of the keys. When was the last time she'd seen them?

Of course, the night she'd arrived. No wonder she'd forgotten. *I must have left them in the ignition.* Refilling her purse, Faith headed to the kitchen.

She used only enough time to spread cream cheese onto a bagel. Today was not a day to run late, especially with the twenty ounces of water she needed to consume to prepare for the ultrasound. Already her full bladder was making itself felt.

Pushing the front door open with her shoulder she found Nick leaning against the front porch railing. He looked much too relaxed and casual. Faith spotted her car keys dangling from his tanned fingers.

"Morning, Faith." His carefree tone caused her senses to spring to attention.

"I see you found my keys." She made a show of looking at her watch as she reached for the keys. "Guess I'd better be going."

He raised the keys just above her reach.

She'd known it wasn't going to be that easy. "What's the game?"

Nick straightened and offered her an umbrella. "No game. I thought I'd drive you to town for your appointment. This being a new area and all."

His reasoning sounded lame, even to her. "That's not necessary. I have detailed directions."

"I'm driving, Faith. The baby is my business, too."

Ah, the root of his offer. The baby. She had actually begun to believe he offered out of concern for her. The past few days had simply been a pleasant illusion and nothing had changed. Nick's ultimate goal was still the child she carried.

She ground her teeth. "Let's go."

Glancing sharply at her, he frowned. She'd have to be more careful to keep the disappointment out of her voice. Nick shielded her from the drizzle with his umbrella as they made their way to the car. She didn't even kick up a fuss when he opened the passenger door for her. After all, driving in the rain offered no appeal to her.

Closing her door he jogged to the other side and slid into the driver's seat. Raindrops glistened in his dark hair. Unconcerned, he shook them off.

"One rule, Nick."

"That would be…"

"I attend the physical portion of my appointment without you." Faith thought she detected a ruddy blush high on his cheekbones, but decided it must be a trick of the light.

He responded with a curt nod and she settled back for the ride.

Nick concentrated on keeping the car between the lines on the rain-slick roads. It required his full concentration to keep his thoughts on the drive, instead of on the confounding woman next to him. Nick ignored the lure of her delicate perfume. Stuff that distracting ought to be outlawed, especially in the confined quarters of a car. It teased and tempted, acting as a tapping finger on the shoulder of his libido.

Nick hadn't felt focused since he'd first heard Faith's name. First, because he'd been disgusted by the thought of her being pregnant with Steve's child. And, lately, because she intrigued him. He didn't quite know what it was about her that bothered him. But he was determined to find out.

He'd watched her the past few days and it wasn't possible to meld what he thought to be true of Faith with the woman he was discovering. The only thing he felt certain of was that she was pregnant with Steve's child.

Shaking his inner thoughts away, he glanced at Faith. She leaned against the headrest with her eyes closed. The dark sweep of her lashes shadowed her pale cheek, but he doubted she actually slept. It was more likely that she was simply ignoring him. After his heavy-handed announcement that he'd be driving, Nick didn't blame her. Wanting to be a part of this pregnancy had caused him to act heavy-handed.

After the night she'd shared the baby's movements with him, actually placed his hand against her body, it had all become real. The baby became more than a possession to battle over. Now it was part of him. By sharing that moment, Faith had become more than his brother's former lover. She was a flesh and blood woman—the woman who carried a Harrison nestled in her body. For a fraction of time he'd have given anything for it to be his.

Things were rocketing out of control.

Watching Faith charm Emily offered him an unsettling truth, she was going to be one hell of a mother. So where did that leave his grounds for custody?

A shrewd judge of character, Mab accepted Faith into her home. Even trusted her to spend time with her daughter.

Why couldn't he accept what appeared so right on the surface? Because he knew Faith had betrayed her sister—like his mother had betrayed her family.

He tightened his grip on the steering wheel and stared bleakly at the ribbon of road through the windshield. Nick realized allowing his emotions to become involved wasn't an option, no matter what he thought he wanted.

Keeping Steve's baby on the ranch was the only thing that mattered. Not him. And not the woman who carried that baby.

Faith kept her eyes closed and concentrated on keeping her breathing even. Feigning sleep was a coward's way out, but talking to Nick was the last thing she needed right now.

The constant back and forth swish of the wipers was the

perfect backdrop for relaxing. Resisting an urge to peek across the expanse of the front seat, she concentrated on how she'd handle him once they arrived. How could she keep the infuriating man from learning anything he could use against her?

Faith opened her eyes as the car rolled to a stop and the engine's purr faded into the drumming of rain. She studied the low, brick building through the rivulets of rain on the window that gave it a soft, blurred appearance.

She tensed as Nick stepped out and circled around to her door. Faith gripped her purse so tightly her fingers ached in protest.

When he opened her door and offered his hand, she hesitated, knowing the reaction her skin would give when encountering his flesh. Hesitantly her hand slipped into his and he pulled her under the shelter of the oversize umbrella.

He looked into her eyes and gripped her trembling fingers for long seconds. "Ready?"

Faith swallowed and nodded, not at all sure that she'd ever be ready.

CHAPTER FIVE

PAPERWORK. Faith knew it was necessary, but being necessary didn't make it less tedious. The headache lingering on the fringes during the drive was now full blown. What had happened to her early-morning relaxation? Oh, yeah, the long drive confined in too little space with Nick—it was a wonder she hadn't shattered into pieces when he'd helped her from the car. The sensual tension that had swirled about her during the drive had obviously not affected him in the least.

She gripped the pen and initialed the final sheet on the clipboard before returning it to the smiling receptionist. Nick leafed through a magazine, trying to act as if visits to an OB/GYN office were commonplace for him.

Sure, Mr. Calm, Cool, and Collected. I can see through your act.

Only the tapping of his fingertips revealed his discomfort, but she didn't waste sympathy on him. He'd bullied his way into this appointment. Actually, Faith was beginning to enjoy watching him squirm. She'd enjoy it more if she knew she could keep him from following her through the rest of the appointment.

The flowered wallpaper and delicate lamps had obviously been chosen to create a relaxing atmosphere, but the contrast with Nick's denim jeans and cowboy boots only accentuated his rugged good looks. More than one expectant mother was casting envious glances her way.

If they only knew.

A nurse motioned to her. "Faith Kincade?"

She stood. Nick was on his feet instantly and followed her when she walked to where the nurse waited.

"The doctor will see you now. You'll be in exam room three."

They followed the nurse down a short hallway. Stopping at the door marked three, Nick bumped into Faith. She jerked away from the body pressed against her back.

Oblivious to the tension between the two of them, the nurse ushered them into a tiny room. She flashed a smile, placed the file folder into the door pocket, and left them alone. The tiny room shrank to the size of a hamster cage. Faith felt trapped in the airless room.

I will not be intimidated.

She turned to Nick, determined to regain what miniscule amount of control she held over the situation. Rules needed to be set and followed. "When things get...personal...you can step into the hall. No arguments." She angled her chin up and looked him straight in the eye.

"Hey, I'm just the driver. This is your show, remember?"

Rather than sit in the chair she motioned toward, Nick walked to a poster hanging on the back of the door. He studied the anatomical representation of an infant inside the womb.

Perched on the edge of the examining table, she did her best to ignore the curious glances sent her way.

He finally sat down. "Amazing."

"What?" She adjusted the neckline of her blouse, feeling more than a little vulnerable.

"I hadn't thought much about what's happening inside you. What changes a pregnant woman goes through."

Faith felt her mouth drop open in surprise. Still staring at the poster, he missed her reaction.

"Aren't you there when your mares deliver?"

His laughter helped ease some of her tension. "It's not quite the same."

Discreet knocking prevented further conversation.

"Come in." They answered in unison.

A doctor bustled in. Bald and smiling, he stuck his hand out. "Ms. Kincade, glad to finally meet you. I'm Dr. Grant."

Giving her hand a vigorous squeeze, his eyes filled with curiosity when he noticed Nick. "Your doctor filled me in on the specifics of your unique situation. You must be..."

Nick shook Dr. Grant's hand. "Nick Harrison. The baby's uncle." He moved to stand next to her.

His protective gesture was somehow reassuring. She must be more nervous than she'd realized.

"Good, good. It's reassuring to see that Faith has family support." Dr. Grant flipped through the chart he held. "With such a rocky start, emotional help is crucial. Of course, we won't be out of the woods until—"

"Dr. Grant, will we hear the baby's heartbeat today?" She feared the questions gathering in Nick's eyes. Her interruption was too obvious but couldn't be helped.

"I'm hoping that it will be possible. The ultrasound should allow us to hear, as well as see, the baby." He scrubbed his hands at the sink. "It's your lucky day. Our sonogram technician just delivered yesterday so I'll be performing your ultrasound. Why don't you lay back and we'll see if we can get a clear image."

Putting her arms out to ease backward, she warily watched Nick. Why had she agreed to let him come with her? The last thing she wanted to do was expose her abdomen with him in the room. It seemed too intimate a gesture for their relationship. His arm wrapped behind her and rested against her upper back, taking the strain off of her abdominal muscles. Having him here did have its uses—she'd simply pretend he was a brother when she had to pull her blouse up.

Yeah, right, a brother.

"If you'll raise your shirt, please. That's good. The gel will be cool."

Dr. Grant squeezed the clear liquid onto her skin causing her to pull a swift breath into her lungs. Cool was an understatement.

When the doctor turned to retrieve the equipment he needed, Nick bent and whispered in her ear. "Do you want me to go?" Reluctance was heavy in his voice.

She knew he would leave if she asked, but she couldn't dim the hopeful gleam in his deep, brown eyes. "You don't have to. It'll be pretty amazing." *Please, stay and share this with me.*

Relief shone in his eyes and she was glad she'd put a smile on his face. Keeping her emotional distance was becoming pure, unadulterated torture.

Adjusting several knobs on the screen, the doctor turned and placed the transducer against her skin. Moving it in precise increments, a form took shape on the screen. At first fuzzy and indistinct, and finally, clear and sharp, the silhouette of an infant was framed in miniature before them.

Faith gasped as unexpected joy leapt inside her heart. Nick reached down and grasped her outstretched hand, seeming to be as touched as she by the sight. There on the screen was an image of the baby's head with its thumb planted firmly in its mouth. The miracle given form and substance.

In the background, she listened to the gentle cadence of a heartbeat. Soothing. Reassuring. Nick turned away from the screen and met her steady gaze before turning back to watch the baby.

Dr. Grant asked questions while moving the transducer for different views of the womb. "Anything unusual to report?"

She forced herself to concentrate on the questions rather than the cowboy rubbing his thumb along the back of her hand. "No. Oh, I did fall a few days ago."

"Any residual pain or bleeding?"

"None." Faith glanced where her hand gripped Nick's. It felt so good, she only hoped the fetal monitor wouldn't pick up her accelerated heartbeat.

The doctor continued to press for information. "You're still taking your medications and injections?"

"Yes."

Nick's attention seemed to focus on the doctor's words and he turned from the monitor. "What injections?"

She regretfully released his hand. It had been nice to pretend something existed between them for a few precious moments. *Ah, well, back to the real world.* "If you wouldn't mind giving me a few minutes with Dr. Grant?" She felt the tenuous bond they'd formed evaporate into the air. It left an ache in her soul.

Nick looked as though he would refuse. Staring at her for long moments, he finally stalked to the door. Before turning the knob, he spoke to the puzzled doctor. "If there's anything wrong with Faith or the baby, I want to know." The door clicked behind his stiff back.

Faith used the time to clean the gel from her skin with tissues, while the doctor packed the equipment away.

Dr. Grant broke the awkward silence. "Ms. Kincade, your personal life is your business." He rubbed his forehead with his fingers as though pondering his next words. "Just remember stress can complicate things for you, and the baby."

"I'm sorry, Doctor. Things are…uncomfortable right now. Mr. Harrison was unaware of the baby's existence until after his brother's death."

"I gather he is not privy to the complete circumstances."

"Not exactly."

Dr. Grant studied her as though looking for something in her eyes. "What you choose to disclose is up to you. Your medical history is, of course, confidential."

Why did his words make her feel ashamed? She had the best reasons in the world for keeping the information from Nick, didn't she? "Thank you, I'll think about what you've said. Will you ask Mr. Harrison to come back in?"

Opening the door, Dr. Grant motioned him into the room. Nick's expression was grim.

"Everything settled?" He looked from Dr. Grant to her.

She nodded. Why was she feeling ashamed again? It was his fault she was forced to withhold information. Why couldn't she keep from caring about what he thought of her?

Dr. Grant approached the examining table with a measuring tape dangling from his hand. "Why don't we see how much the little one has grown?"

Stretching the tape side-to-side and top to bottom, he entered the information into her file. "Appetite normal?"

"Usually."

He flipped the chart closed. "You can sit up now."

Faith pulled herself upright and noticed that Nick made no move to assist her this time. She had only herself to blame. Pulling her blouse down, she slid off the table.

"Just a moment, Ms. Kincade."

She noted Dr. Grant wasn't smiling, not a good sign. "Yes?"

"I have a few concerns I'd like to discuss."

Nick stepped forward. "What's wrong with Faith?"

He asked about me. She knew it didn't mean anything.

"There's no need for undue alarm. I understand that Ms. Kincade has been under high stress levels the past few weeks."

Dr. Grant consulted the chart. "The baby's growth is lower than I would like at this stage of its development."

Faith concentrated on keeping her voice steady. "What does that mean?" She edged nearer to Nick, seeking reassurance from the only source available.

"Probably nothing. But with the special conditions of your pregnancy, anything is suspect." He cleared his throat. "Your weight gain has tapered off, which isn't good for you or the baby."

Nick rested his hand in the curve of Faith's lower back. "Is there anything wrong with the baby?"

"No, no. The heartbeat is strong. But I would like to see Ms. Kincade's stress levels reduced." Snapping the file closed, he patted Faith's hand. "You concentrate on taking care of yourself. Schedule your next appointment for two weeks from today and we'll see what kind of progress you're making. Call me if you have any concerns before then."

Dr. Grant closed the door quietly and left them alone in a silence that seemed to pull at her. Faith tried to prevent the waves of panic that threatened to overwhelm her but she couldn't meet Nick's eyes.

"Faith?"

She couldn't answer him.

"Look at me."

Reluctantly she met his gaze.

His brows were drawn together. "What aren't you telling me?"

She stared at her clenched hands as she tried to decide how best to put him off. "You know the important points. I'm pregnant and Steve is the baby's father." Grabbing her purse, she spun to face him. "Oh, and for some reason, Dr. Grant is under the impression that my stress levels might be harmful to my baby. Imagine that."

Nick stared at her as if she'd sprouted an extra head, but he seemed to sense her panic and didn't push. "Are we done here?"

"Yes."

Opening the door, he ushered her out. "Let's grab some lunch and fatten you up." At her sharp glance, he justified his word choice. "Doctor's orders, remember?"

Surprisingly, Faith enjoyed lunch with Nick. He turned out to be easy to talk to, as long as they avoided personal topics. They'd actually stayed and talked long after their table had been cleared.

Passing through the gates to the ranch, she felt more relaxed than she'd been in weeks and realized he'd worked hard over the meal to make her feel this way. Even though his main concern was for the baby, Faith still appreciated his thoughtfulness and effort.

As the car pulled in front of the house, Wayne hurried to meet them.

Nick rolled his window down. "Everything okay?"

"I've been trying to page you—"

"Damn, I forgot to take it with me." Nick jumped out of the car.

"Dixie is having trouble, things aren't progressing like they should." Wayne rushed through the words.

Nick leaned into the car window to talk to Faith. "One of the mares is foaling and it's not going well. I'll be down at the barn for a while."

"Can I help?" she offered.

"No, thanks. Go on in and put your feet up."

The two men were gone before she could offer a protest.

She let herself into the house. After changing into jeans and a shirt, she settled herself at the kitchen table. Rest was the last thing on her mind.

Faith worked on bookstore ledgers, using the time alone to her advantage. Absorbed in numbers, she lost track of the time until her stomach growled, startling her into looking around. Twilight was settling around the house.

Nick hadn't been to the house since they'd returned—over five hours ago. Faith hoped the mare was all right. Maybe she'd take sandwiches down to the barn and check on how things were going.

Slapping some sandwiches together, she put them into a bag and added fruit and a couple of water bottles. Slipping into her jacket and boots, she walked toward the barn.

Night sounds surrounded her, soothing and familiar now. The crickets chirp welcomed her and the swish of the gentle breeze stirred the aspen leaves above her head. Enough light remained to help her pick her way over the uneven ground. Light glowed from beneath the barn door as she approached.

Pushing the heavy door aside, the scents of the old barn, warm and gentle, rose to meet her. The sound of voices led her to a hushed stall.

Approaching quietly, Faith peered over the half-door. Nick and Wayne crouched next to Dixie. The mare lay on her side and her body shuddered with each heaving breath. Exhaustion showed in her eyes as her nostrils flared wide with tension and fear. Faith felt a sting of tears in her eyes as she saw the mare's suffering.

Poor thing's scared to death.

The crinkling of the bag alerted the men to her presence and she pulled the stall door open. Wayne nodded a welcome as Nick pushed himself upright and walked to where she stood.

Faith looked up into his shadowed face. "How is she?"

"Exhausted."

She moved closer to the mare. "Is she supposed to lie down?"

"It's not uncommon." Nick followed her with his eyes as she approached the horse. "Some mares pace around, others lie down." He looked at the bag in her hand.

Remembering the reason for her visit, she held the bag up. "Thought the two of you could use some dinner. Nothing fancy, just sandwiches and fruit."

Wayne eased himself up. "Sounds like manna to me."

Each man dug a sandwich from the bag. While they devoured the meal, Faith knelt near Dixie's head. She stroked the mare's nose and whispered soothing words. She noted Dixie's ears perk up at the sound of her voice and easing herself onto the floor, she cradled the mare's head in her lap.

Nick turned from his conversation with Wayne. "That's not a good idea."

"A bit of dirt doesn't bother me."

"It's not the dirt I'm worried about. Dixie's head will hit you in the stomach if she flinches."

She couldn't abandon the terrified mare. "I'll stay alert."

Nick didn't look convinced, but he let it drop and instead turned to Wayne. "Why don't you spend some time with your family. Tuck Emily in. There's not much happening right now."

"You sure?"

"Go on home."

Wayne hesitated a moment before giving in. "Give a yell if you need me." He stepped out of the stall. "Thanks for the sandwich, Faith."

"Anytime. Good night."

In the quiet following Wayne's departure, Dixie's breathing seemed louder. Faith continued to sooth her. Looking up, she could see Nick's eyes glinting in the dim light, but she couldn't read their expression.

"Do we need to call a vet?" She asked out of curiosity, but also to break the pull she felt toward the man watching her with shadowed eyes.

"Her water hasn't broken. I think we'll be able to handle it. If she gets into trouble I have most of the equipment we'll need."

Faith felt a flush of pleasure when Nick said "we." She was staring at him again and searched her brain for something to shatter the intimacy created by the situation.

Dixie took care of it by tightening her body. Her harsh grunt echoed in the stall. Nick crouched near the mare's flank.

"It's okay, girl." He turned to Faith. "Looks like her water broke. Watch her head."

"Do you want me to get Wayne?"

"We'll handle it."

Again, the thrill when he included her. "We?" She was certain he'd be able to hear the squeak of panic in her voice.

"You, me, Dixie. You up to it?" He watched her face and waited for her answer as if it mattered.

She gazed into Dixie's trusting eyes and nodded. One woman to another, so to speak, she'd do her best to help. Dixie groaned.

"You're doing great." She kept her voice low and her words calm as she talked to the mare.

Nick moved behind the horse.

Faith felt the sweat dampening Dixie's coat. "You're sure it's all right? Isn't it taking too long?" She hated to question him, but she was worried about something she knew nothing about.

Nick shot her an amused look. "Just how many times have you played midwife to a horse?"

Blushing, she accepted his ribbing. "I don't know nothin' about birthin' no horses." Her quiet joke eased the tension for a moment.

"I see the legs." Nick's voice was soft, but filled with suppressed excitement.

Faith strained upward, hoping to catch a glimpse of the miracle. She watched his eyes fill with wonder and his lips tipped upward. A desire to touch the fullness of that full lower lip caught her unaware and she looked down before he could read it in her face. "Shouldn't the head be first?"

"Only for people, this little one is coming out like nature intended." He managed to capture her gaze before she could look away again. Seconds stretched into an eternity.

Dixie tensed again and pushed.

Faith offered what comfort she could. Looking the mare in the eye, she encouraged her as she would a friend. "I know it's hard. Come on, girl." Feeling helpless, she looked up and whispered to Nick. "Why isn't it here?"

"Everything's fine. Sometimes it takes a while."

By leaning sideways, she could make out the emerging feet. Now the head slipped out.

Nick's face revealed his exhilaration. "I never get tired of this."

Over the next few minutes the foal appeared, one small inch at a time. Faith suffered absolute empathy with the mare. Torn between the need to comfort and the urge to be near Nick during the miracle, she settled on doing one and wanting the other. Finally the full length of the foal was exposed.

"Is it all right?" Why didn't it cry or whatever baby horses should do?

After wiping the membranes covering the foal's head and nostrils, he answered. "Perfect. It's a colt."

She committed the look on his face to memory, the joy and pride, as though he were responsible for the miracle they had just shared. "A what?"

"A boy, greenhorn."

Dixie lifted her head to take a look at the creature that had fought its way from her womb. Faith leaned back as the mare pushed herself up on wobbly legs. Dixie washed her baby, and once she'd cleaned him, she gave him a gentle nudge.

Nick came to stand beside Faith, absently wiping his hands on a towel. He offered her a hand up and she felt her hand swallowed in the warmth of his. Neither released their hands once she stood. Together, they watched the new arrival.

On his second attempt, the colt raised himself on impossibly thin legs. He was all head and legs. Instinctively he pushed at his mother, seeking nourishment and warmth.

Nick slid an arm around Faith's shoulder and gave her a gentle squeeze. "Thanks for your help."

"No. I should be thanking..." Looking up at him, she found his mouth only inches from her own. Her earlier need to touch him returned, a hundred times stronger with his lips so temptingly near.

Wrapped in a sensual haze, she ignored the warning bells clamoring in her head. When she didn't pull back, Nick's eyes darkened with a feral light and his focus lowered to her mouth.

Yes... No... Please! The hope that he'd kiss her, and the fear that he wouldn't, tumbled through her mind warring with one another.

Turning her so she fully faced him, he offered her the opportunity to reconsider, to be rational. She didn't want to think, just once she wanted to touch danger—to taste it. The pull she felt went too deep and was too untamed to deny.

There wasn't enough air and she couldn't quite catch her breath. Was that the wild pounding of her heart thundering in her ears? Couldn't he hear it?

Raising a hand to his chest, she forgot to breathe. The heartbeat that pounded beneath her sensitive skin was as savage as her own. Even Nick's muscled chest couldn't hide it.

Eyes wide, she gazed up at him. Terrified. Excited. Faith tried to remember all the reasons this couldn't happen. They didn't matter. The past and future didn't exist, only this moment surrounded by the sounds of new life.

She darted her tongue across her lower lip and a low growl rumbled in Nick's chest. Reality nibbled at the edge of the fantasy and she pushed against the arm encircling her shoulders. The arm about her waist tightened—it was persuasive rather than punishing. It was still her call.

The light was blocked as he lowered his face toward her. Nick's lips stopped only inches from her mouth when her eyelids fluttered and closed. When nothing more happened, she opened her eyes. Why had he stopped? Their breaths mingled, warming her skin and sending a frisson of pleasure spiraling up her spine.

"Keep your eyes open. I want you to know it's me." Nick's words sent goose bumps racing along her skin.

Only when his lips finally brushed hers did she allow her eyes to close. There was no doubt who was kissing her, the same man who'd slipped into her deepest fantasies.

The back and forth sweep of his lips on hers was torture of the most exquisite kind. Tantalizing. Teasing. Tempting. He stoked a fire in her belly she'd never experienced before with only the lightest of caresses. Waiting for him to deepen the kiss was driving her out of her mind and he knew it. Why else would he wait?

Faith moaned when his arms released her. She wanted more of his hot, sweet mouth. Instead of pulling away, he threaded strong fingers into the hair on either side of her face. Tilting and holding her head with his hands, he resumed the exploration he'd begun.

Heat built within her and curled around her. The soft kisses and nips weren't enough. Faith wanted more. No, she needed more. Not certain what she sought, she slipped the tip of her finger between the buttons on Nick's shirt. Hot, male flesh seared the pad. Another finger joined the first in touching his skin.

Crisp hair tangled in her fingers and beckoned her to explore. Nick groaned when she fumbled with the top button of his shirt. Startled by her own aggressiveness, her hand stilled.

"Don't stop."

His words, spoken hoarsely against her mouth, acted like fuel on the flames roaring within her. Pressing her gently against the wall, he finally stopped teasing her with seductive half-kisses.

His hands tightened in her hair. "Open for me."

Her lips formed a perfect circle of surprise when she gasped. Taking advantage of her wonder, he slipped the tip of his hot tongue into her mouth.

No kiss had ever affected her this way, making her forget everything and everyone else—making her want to try all of the things she'd only fantasized about in her virgin's bed.

Shy at first, she touched her tongue to his. As she grew bolder her daring seemed to electrify him. He drew her tongue into his mouth and she felt the pull in every inch of her body. Returning the favor, she enticed his tongue with her lips. She was stunned when Nick's hips thrust forward.

Faith opened her lips farther, her tongue tangling with Nick's in an age-old dance. She felt bereft when his questing lips left hers. However, her mew of disappointment changed to a soft moan when he lowered his lips to the sensitive skin below her ear. Goodness, she'd thought nothing could feel as wonderful as his lips on hers.

Arching her body into his, she exposed the length of her neck and offered herself up to him. Trailing fevered kisses, he followed the curve to the base, where her erratic pulse beat. Here, the kisses were replaced with long strokes of his tongue.

Past coherent thought, she slid the rest of her hand inside Nick's shirt. Stroking the firm flesh, a fingertip grazed his nipple. It sprang up, pebble-hard.

Melting, she was fast becoming a molten puddle in Nick's arms. What was he doing to her?

What am I doing to him?

Rolling her head to the side, she felt cool air brush the top swells of her breasts. His clever fingers eased two more buttons loose as her breath caught before it resumed faster than before. Nick's gaze focused on the rapid rise and fall of her flesh with each breath she drew. The lace of her bra barely contained the fullness pregnancy had blessed her with—judging by the fire in the gaze he turned to her, Nick approved of the bounty.

Looking at her with heavy-lidded eyes, she sensed his question and his hesitation. After Devon's rejection, she was terrified that he wouldn't want her.

Please don't pull away.

Keeping her eyes focused on his, she reached for Nick's hand. Closing her eyes for a moment to hide her panic, she reopened them and answered his silent question with action. Lifting his hand, she lowered it to the swell of her breast. It was all the encouragement he seemed to need.

Running his fingertips across her skin, he bent and placed a kiss where she'd placed his hand.

She gripped his shoulders and pulled him closer, wanting something she didn't understand. But knowing only that this man could give it to her.

Nick pulled his hand back long enough to slip another button on her blouse through its hole. Pushing the fabric away with the back of his hand, he brushed her nipple with his knuckle. It puckered even tighter.

Faith couldn't stop the heat that burned in her face. No man had seen her like this—she'd never wanted a man to see her like this. Nick's eyes narrowed and his hand stilled.

Drawing a ragged breath, he pulled her shirt closed and buttoned a button. Faith blinked with confusion and hurt. What had happened? What had she done wrong?

Embarrassed, she turned her back to him and finished buttoning her shirt with fingers that trembled. She heard the rustle of cloth behind her as he buttoned his own shirt.

What had she been thinking? Obviously she hadn't. This was Nick Harrison. The man who'd accused her of sleeping with her sister's husband. The man who wanted to take her baby. He must be having a good laugh. She'd just proven his theory concerning her lack of morals.

Straightening her shoulders, she turned to face him. As she opened her mouth to tell him what she thought of his experiment the expression on his face stopped her cold.

Dark as thunder, and twice as menacing, he looked at her with a scowl. The fists at his side clenched. Opened. Closed. Opened. Closed.

"I…" Faith stammered, uncertain what to say. What possible explanation could she offer? She didn't understand her actions. How was she supposed to explain them?

"Go back to the house." His terse words were more intimidating than if he'd shouted.

Humiliated, she turned to leave. His next words stopped her.

"There's a lock on your bedroom door."

She didn't understand what he wanted. "Yes?"

"Use it."

Turning to face him, she was stunned and confused. His back was toward her. Surely he didn't mean—

"Go!"

Faith fled the barn. After she prepared for sleep in her dark, cool bedroom, she turned the lock. But no lock could keep her safe from her own thoughts. She lay in the dark and relived each passionate moment with Nick.

Heaven help her, she hadn't wanted him to stop.

CHAPTER SIX

NICK tried to squelch his raging libido by cleaning the stall. His thoughts were held at bay only by the sheer force of his will. Working around Dixie and the colt, he was careful not to startle them with any sudden movements.

Watching the mare and her new foal, his thoughts returned to Faith. She had helped with the birth without losing her composure—*that* she hadn't lost until he'd touched her. *So much for keeping my mind off her.* He was a bigger fool than he'd realized. What had caused him to reach for her?

Pitching the fresh shavings onto the stall floor with more force than necessary, he looked up to find Dixie staring at him.

She probably sensed his anger. Wanting to avoid stressing her, he approached with a cube of sugar in his outstretched hand.

"It's okay, girl. That's a great looking boy you've got there."

He patted her neck. Yeah. What was Faith carrying in her lush body? A son or a daughter? Steve's child. How could he have forgotten that for even a second? Heart-stopping lust was no excuse for going blind.

Nick admitted, if only to himself, that he'd lusted after Faith since he'd spotted her in Burns's office. His body had a mind of its own where she was concerned. News of the child she carried had cooled him, but only temporarily.

Her soft, innocent eyes had pulled him in tonight. Faith's response had seemed hesitant, almost virginal. What a joke. Irrefutable proof otherwise had pressed into him while he'd ravaged her. Even that reminder hadn't mattered. Once he'd tasted her mouth and heard her moan, he'd been lost.

Reality had pulled him back and stopped him from making the biggest mistake of his life. Because that's what getting involved with Faith Kincade would be. A mistake.

He wanted Faith and would have taken her pressed against the stall boards. Feeling his jeans tighten at the memory, he slammed his open palm against the wall.

It wasn't Faith. She'd simply been there and willing—any woman would do. Randy as a stallion kept from a mare in heat, he needed to stop living like a monk.

Right. Maybe if I think it enough I'll believe it.

Closing the barn door, Nick jumped into his truck and revved the engine. He needed to go for a drive and get this frustration out of his system.

Speeding past the house, he glanced at Faith's darkened window. Who was he kidding?

Faith sat up in bed. The roar of Nick's truck was unmistakable in the silence of the night. He was driving too fast. Remembering the animosity in his parting words, she wondered why she even cared and flipped the bedside lamp on.

Sleep was a futile goal. Hanging her legs over the side of the bed, she reached for her robe and slipped her arms into the silken folds before padding across the room. Stopping in front of her favorite picture of Steve and Carrie on their wedding day, she stared at their smiling images.

The laughter she'd captured on film seemed to echo in her mind. The ceremony had been simple. None of Steve's family present, of course, and only herself for Carrie. The minister had agreed to meet them at a park in the foothills where they'd pledged their love to each other. Till death do us part. But even death hadn't separated them.

Dashing tears from her cheeks, she turned from their picture.

What am I doing?

She was letting them down by giving free rein to her selfish desires. Desires for the one man that she couldn't—shouldn't—want. It would be so easy to blame what had happened on hormones or on her grief and anxiety, but she couldn't. Never at her most hormonal had she been anywhere near tempted to consummate her relationship with Devon. And he'd been her fiancé for heaven's sake. Maybe she was the harlot Nick believed her to be.

Faith knew that was too simplistic—the coward's way out. Brushing the curtain aside, she stared into the darkness with unseeing eyes. Squeezing her eyelids closed, she replayed those frenzied moments of passion with Nick.

Her wanton reaction to him both shocked and bewildered her. Just the memory of his seeking mouth caused her body to clench. No kiss had ever set her blood racing like those she'd shared with him.

Faith had been kissed before. But she had never felt the need to take it further. She'd never allowed things to get out of control. Until tonight.

Nick had smashed her defenses with one smoldering look. Who could blame her? The man was sexuality personified— raw, animal magnetism in denim.

This situation was not going to work. She couldn't stay in close proximity to him. Her lawyer had to find a solution to this nightmare. A way that allowed her to keep her baby while protecting its birthright. A way that took her as far from the baby's uncle as she could get. Before he consumed her and her heart was singed.

Faith settled herself into the comfortable wing-backed chair and tucked her feet under her robe. Straining to hear the sound of a truck's engine, all she heard was the stillness.

Where was Nick?

Faith lingered in her room the next morning hoping to avoid Nick. The night had seemed interminably long and she'd slept only in small increments. Hunger finally drove her toward the kitchen.

She rotated her neck trying to relieve the stiffness. Spending the night in a chair had proved to be uncomfortable and she'd never heard Nick's truck return. Not that it mattered. Where he spent his nights was his business.

Then why do I feel wounded? Bruised? Humiliated? Because she was a first-class idiot. What did she care if he'd found other arms to hold him after he'd rejected hers?

Getting away from the ranch was essential. She had to get on with her life and make a better life for the baby.

Faith entered the kitchen and froze as she felt the blood drain from her face. Nick watched her over the rim of his coffee cup as though he hadn't a care in the world. But the circles under his eyes suggested otherwise.

Steeling herself, Faith remained silent and walked past him. She concentrated on keeping her hand steady while she made herself breakfast. Tension thickened the air and she kept her back to Nick purposefully.

"We have an appointment this morning."

Carefully setting her glass on the counter, she turned to face him. "What do you mean, *we?*"

"I've been on the phone with my attorney the past couple hours. He has contacted Mr. Burns for you." His gaze never wavered from her face. "We'll be meeting them in town at eleven. I thought that would be easiest."

She felt the room tilt and right itself as she stared at Nick in disbelief. It couldn't be true, he intended to use last night's lapse against her already.

"Why?" The word came out as a strangled whisper. She hated the sound of panic in her voice.

"You know why as well as I do." His gaze was emotionless and steady.

Numb, she nodded. She knew why all right and turned from him so he wouldn't see the hurt in her eyes. The response Nick had elicited so effortlessly last night would be her downfall. Judged to be a woman of low moral character, he wanted the custody issue settled. Now.

"I've already spoken to Wayne. He'll cover things while I'm gone."

Faith checked her watch. Two hours wasn't much time to prepare for battle. But then, how much time would ever be enough?

In an attempt to return to her room—her haven in this house, she passed by Nick and gasped when he gripped her wrist. He had to feel her pounding pulse as steady pressure from his hand forced her to turn and face him.

"Don't you have anything to say?"

"Say?" She yanked her wrist free and rubbed where he'd touched her. As though she could erase the feel of his fingers on her traitorous skin. "What do you want me to *say?* That I'm overjoyed with the idea of you trying to take my baby?"

Nick's expression remained unreadable.

"What makes you think you'd be so great for the baby? Look at your family history!" She lashed out again, wanting him to hurt as much as she was hurting.

Nick shoved his chair back and towered over her, his features carved into a dangerous mask. "Watch it. Don't say something we'll both regret."

"Regret? I regret the day I ever heard your name. I regret the day I talked Steve and Carrie into telling you about the baby!"

"What does that mean?"

"I'm talking about how they were driving here to tell you about the baby." She was too incensed to care about the fury building in his eyes. "The trip they died making."

Her final words ended on a sob. Horrified, she covered her mouth and tried to back away from him.

With lightning swiftness, he reached out and seized her shoulders in a punishing grip. "Are you blaming me for their deaths?"

Faith swallowed and tried to speak, but she couldn't squeeze words between her frozen lips.

Nick gave her a light shake. "Answer me." His voice was deceptively calm compared to the turmoil she could see in his eyes.

"No." Emotion choked her. "It's my fault, don't you see? I told them to come, begged Steve to include his family." Her voice rose. "It's my fault!"

Seeing his stunned expression, Faith wrenched free of his

hands and fled toward her room. Slamming the door, she turned the key in the lock.

Burying her face in between her shaking hands, she sobbed silent tears.

What have I done?

Shocked, Nick didn't respond to Faith's words and didn't follow her when she fled the room. Ran from him. What was it she'd revealed? The angry words had flown so fast. He needed time to sort through them.

She'd said "they." Steve *and* Carrie. Both were traveling to tell him, to share the news about the baby. Things didn't add up, pieces were missing. Faith was the key to those pieces, but how could he get them from her?

When Faith emerged from her room, she was subdued and composed. Ninety minutes of soul searching had helped her put things into perspective. No one was going to take this baby.

If she felt threatened by whatever Nick planned today, she knew what she had to do. Her suitcase was packed and pushed into the back corner of her closet. She wasn't a prisoner and could leave at any time. Would leave, if necessary. She'd sever all connections to the past and would go where no one knew her to raise her child. Thus, fulfilling her promise, her responsibility to Carrie and Steve and to the child she loved.

Calm now, she searched for Nick and found him waiting on the porch swing—his face was tense and drawn. Standing, he approached her. He scanned her features, certainly finding evidence of tears. But, also, she was certain, a firm determination. Faith would no longer play the victim in this melodrama. She no longer cared what he read on her face.

"Do you want to ride together?" She moved toward the porch steps. "Or shall I follow?"

Her detached air raised questions in Nick's eyes. Good, she'd let him wonder for a while.

He recovered quickly and followed. "Together."

Twenty minutes later, they stopped in front of a Victorian-style house. The sign on the lawn identified it as a law firm.

Maintaining their silence, Nick opened Faith's door. She ignored his hand and used the door handle to pull herself out. She was determined to be self-sufficient. Lifting her chin, she met his stare.

Bring it on, cowboy.

Walking up the sidewalk, she ignored the heat of his gaze boring into her spine. They entered the front door and passed into a reception area. A perfectly coiffed woman stepped from behind the desk to greet them.

"Miss Kincade, Mr. Harrison. Your attorneys are ready for you. If you'll follow me." She led them down a hallway.

Faith followed, not bothering to see if Nick was behind her. She could tell he was close by the raised hairs on the back of her neck.

Opening the huge door in front of her, Faith stepped inside. A massive mahogany table commanded the center of the room with four chairs flanking it. Two on either side.

The battlefield.

Mr. Burns rose from one of the chairs and shook her hand. "Ms. Kincade, you're looking well."

She watched as Nick greeted his attorney with a handshake and a firm pat on the shoulder. Then he took a stack of papers from the man and flipped through the pages.

Faith returned her focus to the spectacled man next to her. "Mr. Burns, what is this meeting about?"

Shifting, the attorney avoided her eyes. "Mr. Harrison hasn't mentioned the details to you?"

"The only thing he mentioned is the time we needed to be here. And that was only two hours ago."

"I see, well, I'm not certain…that is…we should wait until his attorney has presented…"

Frustrated by the unfinished explanation, Faith turned to face Nick. He approached the table with his attorney. Taking a seat across from them, she waited.

"Miss Kincade, I'm Roy Hatch. Mr. Harrison's attorney."

The man stood and offered his hand. Returning to his seat after she'd accepted his gesture, Mr. Hatch glanced at Nick.

Nick nodded, but kept his attention focused on Faith.

She noticed that Mr. Burns finally sat next to her.

"This meeting was called by Mr. Harrison's request. Having explained some of the circumstances of the situation, he has devised a possible settlement."

She'd just bet he'd come up with a devious plan. "What do you mean a 'settlement'?" Faith turned to her attorney, hoping to find some answers.

"All you need to do is review the option offered by Mr. Harrison. It will be your decision to accept or reject it."

Great, even my attorney is talking in riddles.

Faith pressed Mr. Hatch. "Exactly, why am I here? What option, settlement, whatever, are you talking about?"

"In regard to the possibility of a custody battle for the unborn child," Mr. Hatch explained, "my client is offering an alternative. One he feels, and I agree, that would be in the best interests of the unborn child."

"I don't understand. What possible solution benefits everyone involved?" Faith wrinkled her brow in confusion.

"Mr. Hatch, perhaps it would clarify things for my client if she could review your written offer." Mr. Burns accepted the papers across the surface of the table.

Leaning closer to her attorney, Faith started reading. Halfway down the page the meaning crystallized. It was clearly spelled out in black and white.

She laughed—it was the only response suitable. Nick's face showed surprise at her reaction—it was obviously not what he'd expected. Surely he hadn't believed she would take this seriously. His set expression showed he did.

Looking from her attorney to Mr. Hatch, Faith sobered. This was actually a serious consideration by everyone involved. Except her.

She spoke directly to Nick. "A prenuptial agreement? How does this affect anything?"

"I'm offering a way to avoid a custody battle. To do what is best for the child."

"You're suggesting we *marry?*"

He met her gaze steadily. "Yes."

"You're out of your mind."

"Probably."

"What makes you think I'd lose a custody fight?"

"What makes you think you'd win?" Nick countered.

He knew her deepest fear and played on it, threatening her with the one thing that scared her to death. The possibility of losing her baby.

She decided to call his bluff. "What you're suggesting would never work."

"Why?"

"A marriage of convenience for the sake of a child?"

"It's better than some reasons I've heard of for marrying. Can you think of a more important one?"

Yes, she wanted to shout. Love. Respect. Trust. But none of those came under his heading of appropriate reasons.

She glanced over the papers again and turned to her attorney. "Realistically what are my chances of losing a custody battle?"

"I can't predict that, Miss Kincade. There is a real possibility Mr. Harrison could receive, if not full custody, at least partial. The child could conceivably be caught in a tug-of-war between the two of you for years."

Years. What kind of emotional damage would that cause her baby? She could stall, retrieve her suitcase, and run. Spend her life, and the child's life, in hiding. Always waiting for Nick to find them. Was that fair to the child? Didn't the baby deserve to know its father's family?

Faith massaged her temple. All eyes were focused on her as they waited for her to make the biggest decision of her life. A loveless marriage? To a man who set her heart pounding whenever he touched her. It wouldn't work.

Somehow, Nick seemed to sense her withdrawal. "What is it going to be? Are you willing to risk losing the baby?" He pulled out all of the emotional stops. "What would Carrie and Steve want you to do?"

CHAPTER SEVEN

THE baby's welfare was what it all boiled down to. What *would* Steve and Carrie want her to do?

Faith knew they never expected her to enter into a loveless marriage for the sake of the baby, especially to a man who disliked her. But she also knew they'd wanted the best for their baby. Would endless court battles be best? Would alienating their child from his heritage be what they wanted?

The three men waited.

Deciding to carry the baby for her sister had been the easiest decision of Faith's life. Her heart had been involved. Could she marry Nick knowing he didn't respect her, much less love her? She needed to make this decision with her head, because her heart certainly wasn't involved. Was it?

Examining Nick through her lashes, she admitted there was an intense physical attraction. But would that be enough?

Finally, she cleared her throat and three sets of male eyes focused on her. "I'll need some time to think and decide."

"I'm afraid that's not possible." Mr. Hatch flipped through the papers he held. "If you will turn to page three of the document, the fourth paragraph."

As Mr. Burns turned pages, she searched for the passage referenced.

Mr. Hatch continued. "You'll find that there is a time constraint attached to the contract."

Faith slammed the table with her open hand. "A limited time offer? This is my life we're talking about, my baby's life!" She glanced at the paper again. "Two o'clock—today?"

Nick nodded.

"But that's only two and a half hours away."

"My client feels it imperative a relationship be well established before the child is born," Mr. Hatch explained. "As you are only a few weeks from your due date, this would allow time for adjustments."

She chewed her lip. "When would the ceremony take place?"

"Miss Kincade, our terms are clear." The attorney glanced at Nick. "The deadline *is* for the ceremony."

"Excuse me? I thought that was for an answer. That's not possible. Aren't there blood tests and paperwork?" Faith threw any obstacle she came up with.

"Waived." Nick spoke softly, as he would to calm a spooked horse. "Judge Nelson signed the papers first thing this morning because of the extenuating circumstances. You can have your blood work forwarded from Dr. Grant."

She shook her head. Unbelievable. His terms. His town. She was determined that this baby would have the best shot she could give it, but Nick Harrison would hear some of *her* terms first.

"Let's get something straight. I have terms I want added to this prenuptial before I sign." She motioned to Mr. Burns. "Please write these down, so they can be amended before the ceremony."

Mr. Burns's eyes widened. "You're accepting this offer?"

"Yes." Faith stared grimly at Nick. "I'll accept Mr. Harrison's proposal, with the addition of terms of my own. Agreed, Nick?"

"Let's hear them." He looked skeptical.

"First, I will maintain my own rooms at the ranch." She saw Mr. Hatch's eyebrows lift. Nick's mouth tightened as though he held his words in check. "Second, I'll travel one weekend a month to manage my bookstore. The baby will accompany me on those trips."

Mr. Burns stopped writing. "Anything else?"

"You bet. If the ranch is to be my home, I want to be able to change things around the house." She cut Nick off before he could object. "Don't worry, I'm not planning to knock walls out."

He only shrugged. "Fine."

All right, Mr. Calm, Cool and Collected, take this!

"Finally, but most importantly. As Mr. Harrison has elected himself the father figure for this baby, he needs to start right away. We'll attend childbirth classes together."

Nick leaned toward his attorney for a few whispered words, then straightened. "I'll accept your terms. The revised agreement will be drawn and ready for your signature."

"Should we meet here?" Faith asked.

"No. The minister at the Baptist church agreed to perform the ceremony." He jutted his chin at a stubborn angle. "*That* is not negotiable."

Faith worried her lower lip. Married in a church. It made it seem more personal and almost sacrilegious for a business arrangement. She didn't like the idea, but she'd live with it.

Mr. Burns offered to take her to lunch, food was the last thing on her mind but she knew she'd force something down for the baby's sake. The attorney pulled her chair out as she stood.

"I have a final term to add." Nick's words caused them to pause.

"What?" She didn't feel like hearing any more.

"Find yourself something to wear that makes you look like a bride. The child will expect to see pictures someday. Mommy should look like a bride." He reached toward his wallet.

"Don't even think about it." Faith's voice was laced with steel. "I'll buy my own dress. And if I want to show up in candy-apple red, I will."

Not waiting to hear his reply, she stormed out. Once past the front doors, Faith stood on the lawn and took deep breaths. She didn't like being manipulated and hated this feeling of vulnerability. The terms she'd demanded only offered her a moment's satisfaction, because Nick had won the battle. She knew it, and worse, *he* knew it.

The fact was she was getting married in less than two hours. For all the wrong reasons. To Nick Harrison. Why couldn't he be an unattractive ogre instead of so handsome his hands ignited flames whenever they touched her skin?

Faith made a silent vow that she'd never offer him the opportunity to touch her again. A man who didn't respect her, didn't trust her, wouldn't have her body.

Or her heart.

Faith spotted a dress boutique across the street and glanced curiously through the window.

Seeing a pay phone nearby, she hesitated. Should she call Laura? Her friend would go ballistic, probably try to talk some sense into her through the phone. No. Better to beg forgiveness after the deed was done.

A bell rang when she entered the dress shop. She saw the shop was empty and was relieved to have the privacy.

A smiling saleslady approached. "Good afternoon. Can I help you find something?"

"I need…that is…I'm getting married," Faith stammered.

The woman glanced toward Faith's pregnant middle. "When?"

"Actually, in about an hour."

Startled, the woman turned to the nearest rack. "Goodness, dear. I'll do my best. I don't usually carry much maternity." She looked her over again. "But you're small, except for…any particular color?"

Against her better sense, Faith answered, "White."

Turning to face the mirror, enormous eyes reflected back at her, too large in her pale face. It was time to choose a dress.

With the saleswoman's help, Faith found it. She couldn't help but smile with shy pleasure at her reflection. Off-white with royal-blue trim, the dress was made for her. The high, empire waist camouflaged her advanced pregnancy.

"Oh, the blue emphasizes your eyes. I think there may be shoes to match. What size do you take?"

"Probably a seven, but you don't need to—" Faith stopped as she realized she was speaking to empty air. Playing fairy godmother, the woman had disappeared on her quest for slippers.

Turning back to the full-length mirror, she checked her side-view. Not too obvious. The fabric flowed gracefully to swirl about her calves.

Faith tugged upward on the bodice, but it was no use. A generous amount of cleavage was exposed by the sweetheart neckline. There was no way to help it and she already loved the dress.

"Here we are—slip these on. Only a one inch heel, nothing to upset your balance."

Faith slipped her feet into the delicate shoes. Perfect. She shook her head sadly, somehow finding the right outfit emphasized how wrong this wedding was and canceled the small amount of joy her appearance brought.

"Do they pinch, dear?"

"Oh, no, they're exactly what the dress needs." She couldn't explain the true circumstances of the ceremony.

"Shall I box these things for delivery?"

"If you can help me remove the tags, I'll wear them straight to the church. But it would help if you could have the clothes I wore delivered."

"No problem."

Faith completed the transaction and left her address. Thanking the woman, she turned to leave.

"Wait!" The woman hurried toward her.

"Yes?"

"Every bride needs pearls." She opened her hand to reveal a pair of delicate earrings. "To complete your outfit. My mother always said a bride should wear pearls on her wedding day because it brings good luck." She smiled. "Please accept them as my gift to the bride."

Resisting the urge to refuse the lovely gift, Faith walked over and gave the woman a light hug. Luck was something she was in short supply of these days.

"You have no idea how much this means to me." She put the earrings on. "Especially today."

Seeing the blush of pleasure on the kind woman's face, Faith was glad she'd accepted the gift. She waved once again and stepped out into the warm afternoon sunshine. Everything appeared ordinary on Main Street.

Leaving the store behind, she walked toward the church where her future waited. And her baby's future.

Thankfully the Main Street of Juniper consisted of only two blocks. Both sides were lined with brick storefronts and quaint homes. Faith was glad that this piece of Americana seemed to have missed the urge to turn modern. Somehow, it retained an ageless charm.

The mild day offered the townsfolk a chance to enjoy a leisurely pace. She strolled and absorbed the sights and sounds of small town life, all the while trying to keep her mind off the ceremony that lay ahead.

Since there was no sense in avoiding the inevitable, she turned toward the church. Only thirteen minutes remained until the ceremony was scheduled to begin.

I don't want to keep the eager groom waiting.

The white, stone church sat back from the street. Sheltered among aspen and pine, it represented sanctuary to most people. Faith viewed it as a portal to a life sentence. A life tied to a man she'd never understand. Her steps faltered.

I can't do this. It's madness.

She decided to run for it—just grab her suitcase and go.

The front door of the chapel flew open. Emily ran out the door, straight at Faith. Why in the world was the child here? If Nick had confided in Wayne and Mab, she decided she'd back over him with his own truck. No jury in the world would convict her.

The last thing she wanted was for Wayne and Mab to stare at her with pity in their eyes. She didn't want to lose her friendship with the woman who'd become so dear to her.

"Miss Faith, Miss Faith." Emily grabbed her hand. "Uncle

Nick said you'd want me to be your flower girl. Can I? Can I?''

"Emily, I..." Faith hesitated. She didn't want to see the glowing face looking up at her turn to one of disappointment. "Honey, I'd be honored if you'd be my flower girl."

Emily ran back inside. "Mama, Mama. It's really true. I'm the flower girl."

Faith shook her head. At least one person was excited about the ceremony. She looked up to discover Nick headed toward her with grim determination in each step.

Ah. The anxious groom.

"Where have you been?" Nick ran his fingers through his already disheveled hair.

"Meeting one of your terms." Faith watched his eyes fill with confusion. "The dress."

He shifted his focus and his dark gaze swept over her, lingering on her neckline.

She felt naked beneath his penetrating stare. "It's the only...I mean the saleswoman said I...forget it. It's not as though it matters."

Noticing Nick's clothes, she felt awareness coil within her. He'd replaced his usual snug denim with a dark suit. The fabric did nothing to conceal the breadth of his shoulders. How could the man look good in anything? Faith tore her hungry eyes from their perusal and stepped around the object of her scrutiny.

"Faith."

Reluctantly, she faced him. "Now, what?"

"You look beautiful. The dress is perfect." Nick moved next to her and lowered his voice. "Wayne and Mab are inside."

Her eyes widened and she couldn't keep the hurt from her voice. "You told them?"

"Of course not. We're the only ones, besides the attorneys, that need to know." He glanced toward the church. "I'd like to keep it that way. Let them believe it was a fast courtship, we didn't want to wait. Mab's a romantic so she'll be inclined to believe it.''

Surprised by his regard for Wayne and Mab's feelings, Faith touched his sleeve. "So we go through this like a love-struck couple?"

"Too much of a stretch?" Nick muttered.

"As a matter of fact, yes. But for Mab, Emily, and Wayne I'll give a stellar performance." She hesitated a moment before slipping her trembling hand into the crook of his elbow.

He glanced at where she touched him and covered her hand with his own. "Thank you."

They entered the sanctuary with her hand gripping his sleeve. Faith shivered as the cool air washed across her heated skin. Mab hurried toward them with her arms outstretched. She released Nick's arm and accepted the hug.

"Faith Kincade, shame on you." Mab stepped back. "I know we haven't known each other long, but you could have dropped a hint."

"It happened so quickly I've hardly had time to absorb it myself." Faith looked at Nick with what she hoped Mab would consider loving eyes. "I'm not sure who's more surprised. Me or Nick."

"Emily bounced clear to the ceiling when he called with the news." Mab turned to face Nick. "Nick Harrison, I want you to take a good look at your bride."

He focused a puzzled gaze on Faith.

Mab continued, "She's a vision any man would be proud to have on his arm. And she's just as lovely inside." She waved Faith's protest off. "And Faith…"

Faith raised her eyebrows.

"Nick is rough on the outside. Don't look at me like that, Nick, you know it's true. But, Faith, he's pure gold inside. You'll just have to dig through a bunch of manure to find it."

Nick's outraged expression caused the two women to laugh, and Faith gave Mab a grateful hug before walking to the back of the church. Sunlight streamed in through the open door like the proverbial light at the end of the tunnel. Freedom. All she had to do was keep going. Escape. She stopped inches from the door.

She'd promised to do whatever was necessary to keep this baby. It was time to fulfill that promise. Instead of following her need to run, she turned and faced the front of the sanctuary.

Nick stared at her calmly. He knew of her inner struggle, she saw it on his face and, yet, he hadn't tried to stop her. Either he didn't think she had the guts to walk out, or he trusted her to keep her end of the bargain. Faith wished she knew which, but wondered why it even mattered.

He approached with a cautious smile. "I brought these for you from the ranch." Nick placed a bouquet of wildflowers tied with twine into her hand.

Startled, Faith buried her face in the flowers and inhaled the scent of sunshine. *Why did he pick them?* Her eyes locked with Nick's and she felt the pull of heat between them before she looked away. An attraction to the groom was the last thing *this* bride should be feeling.

Feeling a tug on her sleeve, she looked down at Emily.

Any distraction from her heated thoughts was good.

"Look, Miss Faith." The child held a miniature basket up for inspection.

Faith touched a finger to the collection of delicate rose petals inside. Their sweet aroma wafted upward. "They're perfect." She leaned down and placed a kiss on the tip of Emily's pert nose.

Soft strains of piano music signaled it was time to move toward her future. Squaring her shoulders, she raised her chin.

Emily skipped up the aisle. Rose petals flew through the air as fast as her little hand could liberate them and several of the petals clung to her curls. Faith smiled. Children brought joy in the simplest of ways.

The pianist transitioned into a traditional wedding march— the same refrain thousands of brides walked up the aisle to every day. She placed one foot in front of the other. Had any bride ever been in her position? She hoped not.

Nick's gaze never wavered from her face. Faith glanced to where the two lawyers were seated, both looking doubtful. On the other side of the aisle, Wayne and Mab smiled their encouragement. Emily sat between them, beaming with pride over the job she'd performed.

Faith reached the front of the church and kept her gaze fixed on the front of Nick's jacket, unable to meet his eyes.

"Dearly beloved…"

It began. Faith had attended enough weddings that she could recite the words from memory. But never had she listened so intently, absorbing every word and its meaning.

"Do you take this man to be your lawfully wedded husband?"

She focused on Nick's face. He waited for an answer. Demanded it with his eyes.

"I do." The words were no louder than a whisper of breeze.

"Do you take this woman to be your lawfully wedded wife?"

"I do." There was no hesitation before Nick's confidant response.

"The rings, please."

Panicked, Faith looked at Nick. She hadn't considered this part of the ceremony. His fingers slipped cold metal into the palm of her hand. She looked at the gold band gleaming against her skin. Nick had remembered. He'd thought of everything. She put her flowers down.

Responding to the minister's words, Nick held her hand and slipped a ring onto her finger. Faith grasped Nick's hand with icy fingers that trembled. He steadied her hand and she slipped his ring into place. It nestled in the dark hair sprinkled on the back on his finger. She offered a small smile of gratitude.

"You may kiss your bride."

They stared at the minister. Even Nick seemed to have

forgotten this part, but he recovered and leaned over, his lips pressed a chaste kiss to her cheek.

"Come on, she's not your maiden aunt." Wayne ribbed him.

Nick's jaw tightened and he turned back to Faith; his whispered words were for her ears only. "Here's where we earn our acting awards."

Before she could respond, Nick wrapped an arm around her and bent her back. His other hand cradled her head.

There was no gentleness in his kiss this time. Only masterful possession. He was proclaiming to the world that she was his. For the space of a heartbeat, Faith delighted in his touch and allowed herself to revel in the taste of him. Sanity returned and she pushed against his solid chest.

Pulling back, Nick's eyes glittered with the knowledge that she'd responded. His arm tightened, as he seemed to revel in his power over her. She pushed harder against the well-muscled wall of his chest. He pulled her upright, but kept an arm around her waist as his strong fingers burned through the thin silk of her wedding dress.

"Ladies and gentlemen, may I present Mr. and Mrs. Nicholas Harrison."

Music pounded in her ears and pulled her down the aisle on Nick's arm. Warm hugs and handshakes accompanied the congratulations showered on them. She smiled and spoke, not knowing what she said.

When they prepared to step outside, the minister hurried forward. "One last thing." He held a sheet of paper. "I need you both to sign the certificate."

Nick signed and handed the pen to Faith. She did the same without glancing at the words. It was done. Legal and binding in a court of law. She concentrated on keeping the smile on her face although she was feeling light-headed. Entering into a marriage of convenience could do that to a woman.

Faith stopped pretending to smile as dismay rushed over her in waves. This was too much. Nick tightened his grip and supported her when her legs would have given out.

Walking outside with the others, they headed to where his truck waited at the curb. He opened her door and she lifted the hem of her dress. But when she lifted her foot to the step, she found herself swept off the ground and placed in the middle of the bench seat.

Nick was around the truck and seated next to her in seconds. He slid his arm across the back of her seat as they drove away. Emily's cheering lingered until they rounded the corner and passed out of sight.

Faith scooted as close to the passenger door as possible while Nick chuckled mirthlessly. "Well, your wifely eagerness didn't last long. Guess I can't expect a follow-up on that kiss then?"

She glared straight ahead. "You can go to hell."

"Is that any way for an expectant mother and my new bride to talk?" His sarcasm grated against her raw nerves.

"I may have to be married to you, I may have to live with you," Faith said, "but I don't have to like you." Sharp pain seared through her side. "Oh."

Nick seemed to notice the change in her voice. "What's wrong?"

Faith squeezed her eyelids shut and tried to block waves of nausea as she concentrated on keeping dizziness from overwhelming her. Another pain scorched through her. She doubled, cradling her middle.

Nick slammed the brakes and braced her with his arm while he pulled over. "Talk to me. Where is the pain?" He rubbed her back.

She gasped, unable to catch her breath. "Please…get me to the hospital. Now!"

CHAPTER EIGHT

NICK pushed the truck beyond its limits, as if his life depended on it. Ultimately, it did. If Faith lost the baby he'd never be able to live with himself.

Damn, I knew stress was bad for her. Why hadn't he thought of that instead of his need to ensure the baby stayed at the ranch?

Reaching over, he touched her cheek. It was cool to the touch. Faith's eyes were closed and her breathing shallow.

"I'm going to be sick." Her weak voice rang like a shot in his ears.

Screeching to a halt, he was at her door in seconds to yank it open and ease her out of the truck. To say she didn't look good would have been an understatement. The only color remaining in her face was in her eyes. Eyes filled with misery.

Nick hesitated while she stepped behind a nearby tree. He wanted to go with her, but decided she'd rather be alone.

To hell with it.

Figuring a bad decision beat no decision, Nick found Faith leaning against the tree. If possible, she looked worse. Swearing, he scooped her against his chest and carried her back to the truck. The lack of protest told him more about the seriousness of her condition than her symptoms. Meekness was not a trait he'd have labeled her with in any circumstance.

She let her head rest on the seat.

Nick slammed the door and jumped behind the wheel. "It's only a couple more miles."

He mentally kicked himself as he drove. Where was his brain? His good sense? He'd stood right there when Dr. Grant

101

told Faith to reduce her stress. Coercing her into this sham of a marriage blew the top off the stress scale. If anything happened to the baby or Faith, he'd shoulder the guilt. And the responsibility. Not that it would do any good.

If Steve were still alive he'd kick Nick from one side of the county to the other. Nick knew he deserved it.

"We're here." Tires squealing as he screeched into the lot, he pulled in front of the emergency exit. Lifting Faith from the truck, he carried her through the swinging doors. She didn't open her eyes.

He shouted orders as he pushed through the door. "I need a doctor. Now!"

Several people converged on him. He answered the questions fired at him.

"About six and a half months. She's having abdominal pain." He gently placed her on the bed offered, reluctant to break physical contact, but he stepped back.

Faith opened her eyes and motioned him closer. "Stay." She reached for his hand.

One word. It pricked his guilty conscience. He nodded and her eyelids slipped closed. It wasn't him she wanted, it couldn't be—it was only the comfort of a familiar face in the sea of strangers.

"Sir, we'll need you to authorize treatment if you're a relative."

"She's my wife." Nick signed the requested forms.

"How long has she had the pains?"

"Twenty, maybe thirty minutes. They started right after our wedding."

Two pairs of eyes glanced at him, not bothering to hide their curiosity.

"We were just married. The pains started almost right after we left the church." He hated feeling the need to explain. "Is she all right?"

"If you'll step into the waiting room, someone will come talk to you after we have the lab results."

"No." They'd have to bodily remove him from the room. "I'm staying."

Standing near the head of the bed, he watched the activity swirling around them in the tiny room. Faith appeared to be in the eye of an organized hurricane as machinery rolled into the cubicle.

She opened her eyes when a band was placed around her middle. A heartbeat soon appeared on a miniscule screen.

The nurse smiled. "Good. The baby's heartbeat is strong and steady." She turned to the woman next to her. "What are the stats on Mrs. Harrison?"

"Blood pressure low, but within margins. Pulse steady. Temperature, ninety-nine."

The curtain was pulled aside and a doctor stepped in. He flipped through the pages of Faith's chart. "Let's hook up an IV line." He turned to Nick. "Has she eaten or had anything to drink in the last two hours? Do you know if she's vomited?"

"She was sick just before we arrived. I'm not sure what she's eaten." Nick frowned, feeling powerless and useless. He hated it.

Blood was drawn from Faith's arm and rushed to the lab. Nick stared at a crack in the ceiling as the doctor lifted the sheet and examined Faith and the baby.

The doctor replaced the sheet and stood. "Do you know her obstetrician's name?"

"His name's Grant, she's been to him once. I'm not sure which office." Nick gazed down where Faith now napped.

"I've heard of him." The doctor motioned to a nearby resident. "I need Dr. Grant on the phone."

Faith stirred and lifted her hand. "I'm thirsty."

A nurse placed a cup in Nick's hand. "Only ice chips."

The doctor leaned down. "Mrs. Harrison, I'm Dr. Pembroke. Can you answer some questions?"

"Mrs. Who?" Faith's eyes opened. "Oh, right. Me. Yes."

Nick listened intently while Faith answered the doctor. A

nurse bustled in and handed lab results to the doctor. Another nurse handed him a phone.

Dr. Pembroke took the call. Nick couldn't make out most of the words. The doctor flipped through the chart while he talked and frowned. Nick didn't like that. Doctors should be required to conceal facial expressions.

"Yes, yes. I agree. I'll have the report faxed to you once I've written it up. Thank you, Doctor." The conversation ended with the press of a button.

Dr. Pembroke turned to Faith and Nick. "Well, Mrs. Harrison. You gave us a scare. Especially your husband."

She tried to sit up. "Is the baby all right?"

"All indications are good. Strong, and healthy as a horse from all indications."

Faith sagged against her pillow.

Dr. Pembroke continued. "Looks like you picked up a virus. Normally not a big deal. But lab reports indicate you were already dehydrated when it hit. Not a good combination."

Nick watched Faith's face; a frown of worry was on her face. "Then I'll be able to take her home?"

"Under normal circumstances, I'd say yes. Dr. Grant and I concur that given the uniqueness of your wife's situation, combined with the stress she's been warned to avoid, an overnight stay is recommended. We'd like to monitor her and the baby."

Nick frowned. He didn't like it.

Faith spoke before he could argue. "It's okay. I'd like the reassurance of monitoring the baby. One night isn't long." Her eyes pleaded with him.

What could he say? She was here because of him. Stressed and scared. Nick felt like a big enough idiot without adding to her discomfort.

He spoke to the doctor. "She'll have a private room." He interrupted Faith before she could object. "While they settle you in a room, I'll call Mab. And I'd better move my truck before it blocks an ambulance."

Faith nodded. Relief on her face.

Nick headed to the nearest pay phone.

Faith peered around her room. It was hard to believe the difference thirty minutes could make. Where before she'd been lying on a gurney, now she sat propped against several plush pillows. In place of the nondescript beige walls of the emergency room, the window offered a spectacular view of Pikes Peak. Luxury digs compared to downstairs.

Her wedding finery had been exchanged for a hospital gown and the steady beat of the fetal stress monitor eased her anxiety. Faith knew the baby was fine, heard it in the regular beats. So why did she feel guilty?

Because it was her fault she'd become dehydrated. She'd put the baby at risk by ignoring the signals her body sent. It would be impossible to go on if she hurt the baby. Nick would never have forgiven her.

His concern for her had been commendable, but Faith realized the child inside her motivated it. For a few brief moments she'd allowed herself to savor the feeling of someone taking charge and looking after her welfare.

Wake up, Faith. He tolerated her only for the baby's sake. Believing anything else was unrealistic. She'd better get used to it, when it all came down to it she had to rely on herself.

A soft knock pulled Faith from her musings. "Come in."

Nick pushed the door open and stepped inside with her wedding bouquet gripped in his hand. She'd never seen him look uncertain before, it made her want to reassure him.

"I thought these might brighten the room. A nurse found the vase." Awkwardness punctuated his words.

She remained silent.

"I'll put them here." He plunked them down on the dresser. "How are you feeling?"

"Better. The IV worked wonders." Faith scratched her arm. "This tape is driving me crazy, but it's a small price to pay."

Nick eased into the chair next to her bed. "It's a good

thing I called Mab. She was worried when we didn't come back to the ranch.''

Faith stared at him and mentally traced the line of his jaw as he talked.

"She'll be by later with a bag for you."

"There's no need for her to come all the way in," she protested. "I can wear my dress tomorrow."

"Try telling that to Mab. She wants to be sure I'm taking care of you." He stood and walked to the window.

The silence stretched. Faith relaxed against the pillows and allowed her eyes to slip closed.

"You'll have to tell me eventually."

The softly spoken words shattered the quiet peacefulness that had begun to steal over her. "What are you talking about?''

"Don't take me for a fool." Nick walked to the bed. Towering over her, the lamp cast shadows onto his face. "Things don't add up. If there's something wrong with you or the baby, I need to know. I have a right to know."

She relaxed. He didn't suspect, he was only guessing in the dark.

"I'm your husband. Like it or not." He placed his hands on either side of her head. "We've made a deal. Remember that."

Drifting air carried the smell of his skin. "I'm aware of the 'deal' we made." She refused to be intimidated. "Living in the same house, I'm bound to be reminded daily." Faith poked a finger into his chest, needing to move him away before her traitorous body could respond to his nearness. "Don't forget that every decision I've made is for the baby. For Steve's baby."

Nick reared back and his nostrils flared. Her verbal reminder of Steve struck its target and pushed him away, both physically and emotionally.

"It all comes back to that important fact." Nick eyed her derisively. "You're the same as other women. Except you have something I want. The baby." His smile seemed threatening. "Never forget I always get what I want. No matter what the cost."

His contempt sounded in each step that carried him from the room. The silence echoed after he left.

Faith didn't care. It would destroy her if she allowed herself to care. She hardened the defenses around her heart—no man would have the power to hurt her again.

Closing her eyes, she forced her thoughts to be silent and concentrated on the precious life within her while she drifted toward sleep.

Seconds, perhaps hours later, the door opened and she pretended to sleep. There wasn't enough energy in her to battle with Nick again.

"Please, Nick. No more talking tonight."

"Faith?" Mab's voice jerked Faith from her drowsing. "Are you up to a visitor?"

"Of course, come in." Faith pushed herself higher on the pillows. "I'm so sorry you had to drive all the way to town."

Mab walked to her bedside. "Nonsense. I won't have you adding to your stress by worrying about me." She reached for Faith's wrist and checked the pulse.

"They already did that."

"Double-checking. Can't be too careful." Mab smiled. "Besides I'm a busybody—I like to be involved. Wayne says it's just plain nosiness. Where's Nick?"

Faith looked out the window because she couldn't look her friend in the eye and lie. "Gone for some coffee, I think. He'll be back soon. Some honeymoon, huh?" She reached for her glass of water to avoid saying more.

Mab chuckled. "You two have the rest of your lives for honeymoons. Keeping you and the baby well are important now." She motioned to the small case left by the door. "How about I help put your things away? I'm sure you'd prefer your own gown over the wind tunnels they pass out in this place."

Faith laughed. "That would be a definite improvement."

Mab helped slip Faith's nightgown over her head. April

nights in Colorado carried a chill and Faith snuggled into the familiar warmth of her gown gratefully. Mab cuddled her like a child and then opened the door to accept the dinner tray. She coerced Faith into eating most of it.

The sincere kindness and caring were a balm after Nick's callousness. After plumping the pillows for the tenth time and refilling the water pitcher, Mab looked around the room.

"I think I've done all I can. And Emily is not going to sleep a wink until I assure her you're in the pink of health."

"Thank you."

"Oh, bringing the clothes was no problem." Mab turned to go.

Faith drew a shuddering breath. "I'm talking about your generous friendship. You have no idea how much it means to me right now."

Mab turned and stared at her for long seconds, seeming to search for the meaning behind her words. She finally nodded and left.

Comforted, Faith snuggled deeper into the cozy gown. Not quite the traditional wedding night peignoir, it wouldn't tempt a man fresh out of prison.

Faith surrendered to the sleepy tug of sleep.

Nick slipped into Faith's room. Visiting hours ended earlier, but knowing it was his wedding night the charge nurse allowed him up. He'd checked to make sure Faith was asleep when he'd passed the nurses' station.

He'd been wandering the streets of Colorado Springs for hours hoping the exercise would cool him off. The argument with Faith emphasized the challenge ahead. Their disagreements raised her stress and endangered the baby. How were they supposed to build rapport if they attacked the jugular every time they came within three feet of each other?

He stared into Faith's shadowed face. Relaxed in sleep. Soft. He'd learned how tough she could be. Like any female protecting its young.

Her dark lashes emphasized the paleness of her skin. It

was easy to see how Steve had been tempted. She looked every inch the young innocent instead of a she-wolf in lamb's wool.

His father would laugh at him. Not with humor, but with cynicism. The one thing he'd drilled into his sons was the deceitfulness of women. Nick rebelled against those lessons by marrying a woman like Faith. A woman guilty enough to dim his mother's sin in comparison.

It had always been easier to keep his relationships with women on the surface. Sexual. He'd known it was time to move on when a woman looked for more than he could offer. Commitment and marriage weren't part of his life plan.

Until now.

However they'd gotten here, he and Faith were married. Not because they wanted it, but because the life growing within her demanded it. Nick protected and watched over family. No matter what.

Pulling a chair closer to the bed, he settled in for his vigil. He stared at Faith for what seemed like hours before he felt the edge of his tension dull.

After being awake all night and then the rushed wedding, Nick hoped to fall flat asleep on his face. He eased his boots off and propped his feet on the edge of the bed. A comfortable position wasn't likely with his frame squashed into a miniscule chair, but he'd slept rougher.

Nick closed his eyes and lay his head back. He concentrated on relaxing his tense muscles one by one.

"Steve!" Faith's cry shattered the stillness.

Nick leapt out of the chair—his nerve endings on alert. Disoriented, he stared down at Faith, but her eyes remained closed. She tossed about on the bed. He reached out a hand to wake her, but stopped when she spoke again.

"Carrie. I'm doing the right thing, you know I am."

Nick listened intently to the words that were coherent. Beads of moisture glistened on Faith's forehead as the anguished words tumbled between her lips.

"Devon, I can't lose the baby...they won't forgive me... Carrie...Steve... Where are you?"

Her thrashing turned desperate and the IV strained to pull free from her arm.

Nick placed his hands on her shoulders to stop her movements. "Faith." She continued to pull against him. The heat from her skin seeped through the flannel gown and seemed to burn his fingertips. "It's okay. I'm here."

She stilled but continued talking in her sleep. "Steve? What took you so long? I needed you."

Nick ached to pull away and walk out of the room. She'd slipped from her nightmare into a dream. He didn't want to hear more.

She gripped his hand before he could move away. Smiling in her sleep, she placed it against her cheek. "Carrie will be so happy." Peaceful sleep replaced the confusing words.

Unable and reluctant to remove his hand from her silky cheek, he pulled the chair closer with his foot and sat. Faith's words tumbled in his head. Tangled and straightened. They didn't make sense, but who said a nightmare had to make sense? Ramblings didn't have to mean anything or make sense.

A frown pulled at the corners of his mouth as he stared at her sleeping face. He'd figure it out. His thumb stroked her warm flesh of its own volition.

Nick would have to find a way to keep his hands off his wife while he solved her mysteries.

The last webs of sleep scattered as Faith emerged from her refreshing sleep. She was famished.

Stretching her arms above her head, she froze. Both of her hands were above her head so whose hand nestled in the curve of her neck? Faith's eyes flew open and she tried to sort out the extra appendage. Dark hair lay on her pillow—it wasn't her hair. Nick's relaxed features came into sharp focus.

His six-foot frame was folded into a chair and he'd bent at the waist to share her pillow.

She resisted the urge to laugh out loud as the irony of the situation slammed into her. Somehow, she'd shared a bed with her husband. On their wedding night. Not in the traditional sense, but closer than they'd planned.

Taking advantage of the opportunity, she studied Nick's face. With his defenses lowered, he seemed younger. But in no way softer. Even in sleep, his features might have been chiseled from the mountains he loved. Nick Harrison could never be considered soft.

The cleft in his chin drew her gaze. A chin always set at a stubborn angle, as though he had to prove something to the world. And perhaps, himself. Her hand moved of its own volition and traced the stubble along his jaw. Intent on the texture of his skin she forgot to notice his breathing. As her gaze wandered upward, she met his intense gaze.

Oh, my, God. She snatched her hand away from his face.

"Playing with fire?" Nick's voice, husky from sleep, sent a tingle through her. "Didn't your mother tell you fire burns?"

Embarrassed to be caught touching him, she turned away from his suggestive smile and teasing words. His low laugh rumbled through the mattress.

Nick pushed himself upright. "Cheer up. I hear the breakfast cart."

She stared at him. "How did you know I..."

"Your stomach's growling woke me...among other things."

Faith cursed the heat rising in her face. "You're no gentleman."

Nick's smile slipped. "Never said I was."

Faith ran the comb through her hair, amazed at the difference two hours could make. Nick had left when breakfast arrived. Checking on the ranch seemed as good an excuse as any. She knew that's all it was—an excuse to be away from her.

Enjoying the meal and talking the doctor into removing the IV encouraged her. A shower never felt so good. The nurse hovered outside the door while she let the warm water glide over her skin. It refreshed her and helped her feel more prepared to meet the challenge of dealing with her "husband."

Faith fastened her hair into a tight braid. She started at the knock on the bathroom door. "Yes?"

Dr. Pembroke peaked around the door. "I came to see if you'd be interested in going home?"

Faith smiled. "Please."

He pushed the door wider. Nick stood next to him. She stepped into the room, all lightheartedness forgotten.

Dr. Pembroke checked her eyes with a penlight. "Any problems during the night?"

"None." She wondered why Nick stared at her so harshly.

"Everything appears normal. Your hydration is restored, so I see no reason that you can't head home." The doctor turned to leave, hesitated and addressed Nick. "Mr. Harrison, make sure she keeps up a healthy lifestyle. The discharge papers will be at the desk."

Faith squirmed under Nick's stern scrutiny once they were alone. She felt guilty and didn't know why. "I'll just gather my things and we can leave." Faith escaped into the bathroom and leaned on the door after she closed it. Meeting the reflection of her eyes in the mirror, she hardened her resolve. Nothing had changed. Nothing but the date on the calendar.

"Faith?" Nick spoke from beyond the door.

"Hmm?"

"Why would Carrie be happy about the pregnancy?"

She yanked the door open and faced him. "What makes you think she was?" *Act normal, it's just a question.*

"You talk in your sleep. You had a nightmare last night."

"I suppose you stood there and listened?" She planted her hands on her hips. "Didn't it occur to you to wake me?"

"I warned you. If you won't share information with me, I'll get it any way I have to."

She wanted to stomp her feet. "Men! Can't one of you be counted on to do the decent thing?"

Nick caught her hand in his warm grip. "Who was he?"

Faith stilled. "What's wrong? Didn't your lawyer include that in the report?"

"The pale line on your finger told me. I never noticed it before the wedding." He released her hand.

"I used to be engaged, now I'm not."

"How long ago?" He rammed his fists into his jean pockets.

"How long ago, what?" She tugged on the end of a braid to hide the trembling in her hand.

"Your breakup."

"Seven months. And to answer the next question, no he's not the father. It's not possible." She stalked around Nick and shoved her remaining toiletries into her case.

"You're sure?" Nick's tone echoed the doubt behind his words. His distrust of her.

"Unless it was an Immaculate Conception, I'm positive. I think I would remember having sexual relations with a man." Slamming the case shut, she lifted it from the bed.

He blocked her exit and stared at her with unconcealed contempt. "Do you expect me to believe you were engaged to be married and never slept with the guy?"

"I really don't care what you believe."

"What was wrong with the guy? Why Steve, but not him?" He removed the suitcase from her hand. "Did your fiancé know?"

Faith nodded her head. "He knew." *It doesn't matter.* Nick's distrust of women would make it impossible for him to comprehend her motivations. Much less understand them.

Nick Harrison would believe exactly what he wanted to believe of her.

The worst.

A routine was established as the days blended together—a co-existence. Faith didn't know which was worse, outright battle or this uneasy truce.

Since the wedding, she and Nick had been tiptoeing around

each other in a bizarre dance. Exchanging only the most necessary of comments, when they communicated at all.

Faith felt her former life slipping further away, blurred on the fringes of her memory.

But even the strain of her encounters with Nick couldn't diminish the pleasure she found on the ranch. The summer heat had encouraged the trees to develop lush, green foliage overnight and flowers flourished in every unexpected corner. Exploring the ranch showed her the reasons Nick was obsessed with protecting it.

Daily visits with Toffee and the other foals elicited much-needed giggles. Emily accompanied her, a ritual the child never allowed her to forget.

Faith added her personal touches to the farmhouse. Bright curtains replaced the tired ones left by former residents.

Nick shocked her the first night home from the hospital when she discovered him transporting an armload of linens into the room adjacent to hers.

"What are those for?" Faith knew her apprehension was evident.

"My bedroom upstairs is too far away." Nick pushed the door open. "I can't hear you if something happens at night."

"But, I…" She shrugged. What he said made sense. She moved to the far side of the double bed and helped tighten the sheet.

Flicking the top sheet, she snapped it into place. Together, they finished the job.

"I'll grab some more things." He turned to go.

"Nick?" She cleared her throat and continued. "The room across the hall, the sewing room…"

He didn't make it any easier, but stood silent with his arms folded across his chest.

"I'd like to use it for the baby."

Nick's features closed further. "I don't think my mother will be using it. Go ahead."

She resisted the urge to pry, sensing the futility of it. "Thank you."

After lunch, Faith rolled up her sleeves and tied a kerchief over her hair. Today seemed as good a day as any to tackle the sewing room. She pushed the door open and stopped in surprise.

The room stood empty. All traces of anyone erased. Nick had removed everything. Faith wasn't sure how to react. On one hand she was grateful to be saved the work. On the other, Nick's callous rejection of anything associated with his mother bothered her. She cleared her mind and set to work.

Good old-fashioned hard work soon transformed the room into a nursery. Faith was satisfied that the baby would have a peaceful retreat.

Tipping her head back, she smiled. The ceiling she and Mab had designed and painted together—a light blue sky scattered with whimsical clouds. The far wall had been transformed into a forest scene. Woodland animals peered out of shadowed foliage with bright, curious eyes.

She was no artist, but hoped the love used to create the designs made up for the lack of talent.

Mab fussed over her the entire time. Three fans circulated fumes through the open windows and kept Faith from inhaling any scent of paint.

Faith wished she could accept the respite Nick offered. Instead she wrestled with a restlessness she didn't understand. For what, she didn't know.

Crossing to the open window, she lowered herself into the chair she'd dragged from the kitchen. Watching Nick and living with him, revealed facets undiscovered in the man she'd married.

His treatment of the horses was knowledgeable, at times reverent. They weren't a livelihood. They were a passion.

Affection for Emily was evident in the patience he showed her. Endless, silly questions were answered. Chores put on hold for a game of tickle-tag. Faith was convinced he would be great with the baby.

Still, she worried. What would the baby learn from them

and their relationship? Eventually it would realize theirs was not a traditional marriage. She hadn't thought of those possibilities when she'd made her desperate choice.

Restless, Faith tapped her foot and closed her eyes. She wanted her child to experience the same warm childhood she and Carrie had lived. They'd been secure in the knowledge that their parents loved each other.

How could she offer her child any less? What choice did she have? Faith hadn't chanced the slightest risk she might lose custody. Her sacrifice didn't matter.

Impatient with the path her thoughts wandered, she stopped her racing mind with great effort. It was time to stop feeling sorry for herself. Life was the way it was. She'd made a decision and she'd live with it.

Rising from the chair, she headed toward the kitchen. A walk in the fresh air would help regain her focus. The phone rang before she pushed the door open.

She grabbed the receiver. "Hello."

"Are you busy?"

"Nick? Where are you?"

"I'm calling from town. Can you meet me?"

Faith felt the bottom fall out of her stomach. "What's wrong?"

"Nothing. Look, I came to town for supplies and there's something I thought you'd like to see."

Confused, Faith answered, "Sure…where?"

"I'm parked on Main Street. You can't miss the truck. Park near it and we'll walk from there."

The buzzing dial tone confirmed that the conversation had definitely ended. She looked down at the oversize shirt and leggings she'd pulled on that morning. No way she'd show up in town looking like a pregnant housewife. Even if that's basically what she was at the moment.

Faith headed to her room, her heart heavy in her chest. What was Nick up to now? Would she be mentally tortured again? Had he come up with a plan to win custody of the baby? What if his lawyer had accessed her medical records?

Stop it. Get a grip.

They were married. There was no way for Nick to take the baby.

Was there?

She knew better than to underestimate him.

CHAPTER NINE

A CRIB. Nick had invited her to town to shop for a baby bed. Not exactly what she'd expected. Thank goodness.

Running a hand across the smooth headboard, Faith watched him as he questioned the store's owner.

Nick gestured in her direction and the man next to him smiled at her. She offered a polite wave and they returned to their conversation.

When Nick laughed at something the other man said it transformed his face. The white of his teeth emphasized his tanned skin. The baby would be lucky if it inherited the Harrison smile. It filled the whole face. Open. Honest.

"So what do you think?"

Faith jumped as though Nick had read her thoughts. She hadn't noticed his approach and pressed a hand to her neck to concentrate on calming her racing pulse.

Studying the bed, she realized its style was reminiscent of times gone by and the oak finish glowed with warmth. She'd actually noticed it even before he pointed it out and imagined a tiny babe sleeping away lazy afternoons nestled safely inside.

She smiled at Nick. "It's perfect."

He pulled his wallet from his pocket and Faith opened her mouth to protest.

"Don't think of saying anything." His jaw set at a stubborn angle. "I'm buying this. Call it a gift from an uncle if it makes you feel better." Nick approached the register with credit card in hand.

Faith pressed her lips together. What could she say? He deserved certain liberties where the baby was concerned and she needed to let him be involved even if she hated the idea of sharing her baby. Nick was gung-ho now, but what about when it actually arrived? Could she trust him to stay involved? Or would he tire of playing the doting uncle?

Stop it. Assuming that every man was like Devon wasn't healthy and she couldn't assume that Nick would eventually reject the baby.

If only she could convince her heart as readily as her head.

Several days later, Faith listened as a large truck approached the house. Pulling her hands from the sink full of soapy dishes, she grabbed a towel.

A knock on the front door reverberated through the entryway. Faith hurried to answer the summons.

"Morning, ma'am." A large man nodded and extended a clipboard. "We have the furniture your husband ordered."

Faith accepted the clipboard and noted Nick's signature on the delivery order. She glanced up and watched another man approach the back of the truck.

Smiling, she handed the clipboard back. "Please, bring it in. I didn't realize a crib needed a delivery. I planned to stop by the next time I went to town."

The man with the name Hank stitched on his pocket pushed the hat off his forehead and scratched his head. "Ma'am?"

"It seems a waste for you to drive all the way out here to deliver one crib."

Hank checked his paperwork. "There are four items listed on the delivery inventory."

Faith blushed. He probably thought it odd a wife didn't know what her husband had ordered for the nursery. If he only knew…

Embarrassed, she folded and smoothed the dish towel clenched in her hands. "I'll show you where the room is."

The men emerged from behind the truck a minute later with a dresser supported between them. It matched the crib she'd chosen with Nick. Faith ushered them into the nursery and chose a spot for the piece before they headed back out.

Moments later, they returned. Hank carried a changing table and his companion shouldered the box containing the crib. Hank lowered the table and turned to help assemble the bed.

"You don't need to…I mean, I can get it later," Faith faltered.

"It's all part of the service, Mrs. Harrison."

The men assembled in a few minutes what would have taken her hours. The crib was more charming than she remembered. It completed the room.

She followed the men to the front door once they'd finished. "Can I offer you anything to drink before you leave?"

"Thanks, but we carry a cooler. There's still one more item on the truck for you."

Faith had forgotten about the fourth piece. What else had Nick ordered? Hank emerged from the depths of the truck with a rocking chair on his back and she followed him to the nursery, speechless.

Faith nodded absently when Hank wished her a good day. The truck engine faded as it bounced down the drive and she looked around the room. Her focus returned to the rocker. Nick must have seen her admire it. She'd even rested in it while he talked.

Lowering into it, she set it rocking with her toes. It felt as comfortable as she remembered. Nick's thoughtfulness humbled her. Was she wrong to mistrust his every move?

Nick tossed another bale off the truck onto the barn floor and wiped his forehead with a dirt-streaked sleeve. Straightening, he watched Wayne stacking the bales of spring hay into some kind of order.

"Hey," Nick's voice rasped past the dryness of dust in his parched throat. "Let's knock off for a while and grab a cold drink to give our lungs a break."

A cloud of dust and hay particles danced heavily in the afternoon heat.

Wayne yanked his leather gloves off. "No argument here. I'll run home and see Emily before her nap."

Nick watched as Wayne loped toward his house and envied him. For about two seconds. What Wayne and Mab shared was as rare as a two-headed foal. The reality of marriage was that it turned into a plughole that pulled the life out of a man. *Didn't it?*

The truth was Nick looked forward to dinner with Faith at the end of the day. Homecooked meals and overtures of friendship were becoming a staple and that scared him to death.

Nick swatted a fly from his arm and glanced up at the sound of approaching footsteps. Faith walked toward him while balancing a tray in her hands. She was graceful, even this late in her pregnancy. Nick's hungry gaze lowered to her chest, the slight bounce under her shirt teased him.

He shifted as his thoughts relayed into tightened jeans. If he stood, Faith would see exactly how she affected him.

Nick glared into her sweet, smiling face.

Damn the woman.

Faith felt her smile slip. Nick's scowl made her want to turn tail and run for the house. His eyes gave nothing away. She nearly tripped.

Don't let him see how he affects you.

Setting the tray onto a bale near Nick's feet she smiled up at him. She'd gathered the pitcher of sweet tea and glasses the minute she'd seen Wayne head for home.

"I thought you might be thirsty." She didn't risk looking at him while she poured the tea. Finally she risked a glance through her lashes.

The sight of him set her traitorous body tingling. Faith had noticed his gaze on her breasts as she approached, at the unbidden memory they swelled toward him instinctively. She hoped her reaction wasn't noticeable straining against the confining fabric of her shirt.

She held her breath and passed a glass to him. "This

should quench your thirst.'' The double meaning was obvious.

As Nick tipped his head back to swallow a long draw of the refreshing tea, Faith was mesmerized. The column of his throat was exposed to the sun, working as the liquid slid down. A renegade drop of sweat ran under the collar of his shirt and she followed it with her gaze until it disappeared from sight.

Desperately she looked toward the snow-capped mountains in the distance. She hoped the peaks would distract her, but the mental images taunted her. Even with her eyes turned elsewhere, the memory of how the fabric stretched tight across Nick's chest was all she saw in her mind's eye. A slow flame burned inside her, confusing her.

I can't forget who I'm dealing with. Just because he'd starred in all of her sexual fantasies lately didn't make him any less the enemy.

Faith faced Nick with her determination strengthened. It was a mistake. Merciful heavens, what a mistake to look at him again.

Nick was leaning against a bale of hay and wiping his face with a shirt. The shirt he'd been wearing the last time she'd looked. The shirt that had teased her with a hint of what lay underneath. It no longer teased her, the reality of his flesh was revealed.

Faith stared at his tanned skin and drank her fill of the sight of him. With his eyes closed, he unknowingly offered himself for her visual feast. Unashamedly she stared.

Faith wasn't a prude, but her exposure to naked male physiques was limited. And certainly none had enticed her as Nick's bronzed torso did now. Whorls of crisp, dark hair trailed down his chest before disappearing inside the top of his jeans. She jerked her stare from where her imagination led.

Her startled gaze met Nick's. She breathed so rapidly she feared she might be on the brink of panting. Nick leapt off the truck, landing inches from where she stood. Faith took two steps back, maintaining a safe distance from the heat of his body.

"I...I need to get back." Frantic, she reached for the pitcher and Nick's empty glass. The mischievous glass was just beyond her reach.

Stretching to retrieve it, she froze and her breath stopped somewhere near the middle of her chest as a tanned arm reached around her and strong fingers wrapped around the errant glass. She sensed the length of Nick's body only a breath from her own. Faith dared not move, fearing that full contact might cause the burning inside to erupt into flames. Consuming her with its heat.

Nick saved her from making a choice. "Hot?" His breath tickled her ear.

"Wh...what?" She turned to see if he realized what he did to her and found her eyes level with his mouth. His lips moistened from the sweet tea. She swallowed and allowed her gaze to travel upward.

Knowledge was in his eyes. He knew exactly how her body responded to his closeness. Faith looked deeper and saw the flames burning in his gaze. He felt the fire's pull, too.

Both stared. She silenced the logical part of her brain that screamed at her to get away from him. Just once she wanted to act on impulse and her woman's instinct.

Keeping her gaze focused on the desire in Nick's eyes, she licked her dry lips and watched the fire roar in response as he sucked air through clenched teeth. Faith turned back toward the truck and closed her eyes, trying to control the wildfire rushing over her. Finally she surrendered to pure feeling and leaned into Nick.

Her body thrilled when it touched his. Front to back, neither moved. Faith was grateful they were not within easy sight of anyone.

Nick raised his hand and swept the hair from the nape of her neck allowing his hot breath to fan over her sensitive skin. He touched his lips to the skin he'd exposed. Shivers caused her shoulders to tremble.

Faith kept her eyes closed and waited for the world to right itself. For her breathing to slow and her heartbeat to return to normal.

The return of normal respiration brought the return of her sanity. Standing without his support now, she couldn't turn to face the triumph she knew would be in his eyes. She jumped when he reached around her and offered the tray. Nick stepped back to let her pass.

Unable to resist, Faith glanced at his face. Shuttered, his eyes were unreadable and told her nothing.

"Watch it!" Wayne ducked and barely avoided being clobbered by the bale Nick tossed out of the truck. "What's wrong with you? That's the second time you've about knocked my head off my shoulders."

Nick straightened and whipped his hat off. He wiped his face with his grimy sleeve. "Guess my mind's on other things."

"No kidding." He lifted another bale and put it atop the stack before focusing his penetrating stare on Nick. "Was Faith down here?"

"Yeah."

"She didn't stay long."

Long enough.

Nick jumped off the truck. "She brought a cold drink." He helped Wayne stack the bales remaining on the floor.

"Thoughtful of her."

Nick fumed. What in the world could he say? Oh, while she was here I jumped on her like a hormone obsessed teenager. Touched her, as only a husband should. Hell, he *was* her husband. So, why did he feel like he'd taken advantage of her?

He tossed a bale upward and welcomed the strain on his tired muscles. Sweat ran between his shoulder blades.

Wayne leaned against the truck and took a long drink from the water bottle he'd carried back with him. Nick knew he watched him, trying to assess his mood.

"She's getting to you, isn't she?"

Nick froze and aimed a threatening look at Wayne most men would have heeded. He knew Wayne wanted some answers. Too bad he didn't have any for him, he didn't know them himself.

"You have to admit she's easy to look at." Wayne offered him the water. "She's smart and always ready to pitch in."

Nick took a pull from the bottle and let the liquid cool his gut. If only he could extinguish the fire Faith stoked as easily.

"You make her sound like a saint." He twisted his lips in a sneer. "Aren't you forgetting one detail?"

Wayne's brow furrowed in concentration and his lips turned down. "You mean—"

"Yeah, the not-so-trivial matter of the baby she's carrying."

Wayne scuffed the heel of his boot in the dirt and avoided his eyes.

"Steve's baby," Nick continued.

Wayne's gaze locked with his. "You so sure of her? Don't go using the same brush on Faith you use to paint your mother. They're two different women, two different situations."

He laughed without any humor. "What the hell do you know about it? It wasn't your mother running out on you. It's not your wife carrying your brother's child."

Wayne stepped closer to Nick. Years of friendship were tucked under their belts and each had learned how to read behind the other's words.

"Seems to me it wouldn't bother you so much if she hadn't worked her way under your skin." He clapped a hand on Nick's shoulder. "It's hard to see what's under your nose if you keep using tunnel vision the way you do."

Nick watched Wayne turn and leave. Watched until he disappeared from sight. Slapping his hat against his thigh, he shook his head. Just because Faith felt like a fever he couldn't shake didn't mean she was under his skin.

Nick looked at the thunderheads building in the western

sky above the mountains. The afternoon storms couldn't be stopped, so, he'd learned to live with them. Lightning flashed and he counted two beats before thunder reverberated through the air. This one was close. It might prove impressive.

He stood for a moment and absorbed the energy that pulsed in the air. The storm roiling overhead matched the one raging inside him. The one Faith let loose.

CHAPTER TEN

FAITH wakened with a start. She rubbed her eyes and listened as wind driven rain rattled against the windows. Stretching, she relaxed. The storm must have disturbed her.

Standing, she tightened the belt of her robe. Lightning flashed and illuminated the shape of a man. Faith gasped—Nick. The darkness was deeper following the blinding brightness and she gripped the footboard. The next flash revealed that he'd moved closer. She'd closed the door, so why was he in her room?

Her relief at identifying him turned to apprehension. Something must be wrong, it was the only logical reason for his presence.

"What's wrong?" Faith backed away, needing to put some distance between them.

Nothing. No reply. Nick ignored her question and moved closer, his eyes gleaming in the twilight.

The switch to her lamp didn't respond and she groaned silently. Alone in the dark with a man who made her want him, wasn't a good place to be.

"The electric's out." His voice pierced the gloom.

The timbre of his voice tensed every muscle in Faith's body and she resisted the urge to flee. The intimacy of the setting scared her and made her aware of her weakness where Nick was concerned.

Awareness surrounded her. The next stroke of lightning revealed a change in Nick's eyes. It showed that he'd felt the change in the atmosphere as well.

Nick's stare dropped to where her pregnant shape was emphasized by the smooth fabric.

"Was it worth it?"

The change in the conversation confused her. "Was what worth it?"

"Sleeping with Steve. Was it worth the baby? Worth betraying your sister?"

"You boorish, insufferable, self-righteous…" Her mouth worked but no more words emerged.

"I'm not throwing stones. No one's perfect and we both know how responsive you are to a man's touch." Nick's mouth lifted sardonically. "I can see how Steve could lose control and be tempted. Especially with you living under the same roof."

Faith swung her arm toward his insulting face before her mind registered the action. Capturing her hand easily, his grip was far from gentle.

"You have no right to mention his name." She willed herself not to cry. "He and Carrie were everything to me. They were my family."

When she tried to pull her arm free, Nick used it to haul her closer. Her belly pressed into him.

Her eyes widened when his hungry gaze shifted to her mouth. She knew her body would turn traitor to the seductive power he wielded.

Hot breath fanned her cheek. The man scent of him assaulted her senses. The smell of leather and skin a potent combination. More addictive and seductive than any man-made product.

She closed her eyes and accepted the inevitable.

An unexpected jolt startled her. Nick felt it, too. Leaning back, he looked confused. They both peered at where their bodies touched as the baby kicked again.

Nick looked into her eyes. "Your own knight in shining armor."

Faith nodded, grateful that the tension was relieved naturally. They stepped apart and avoided looking at each other. Nick walked to the window and surveyed the skies.

He turned to face her. "You can't keep your secrets forever.'' Nick sauntered to the door and closed it behind him, leaving a gaping silence behind.

''Want to bet?'' She mumbled under her breath and patted her stomach. ''Thanks, little one.''

Shaking her head, Faith pulled clothes haphazardly from hangers. She was determined to be fully dressed for her next encounter with her husband.

Hunger forced her to the kitchen an hour later. The lights were still out. Nick sat at the table where a kerosene lamp cast golden shadows around the room.

She studied him for a moment before entering the room. Dark lashes spiked on his cheeks as he studied the papers spread across the table and his hair lay in damp curls against his head. Day old whiskers gave him a roguish air, half cowboy and half pirate. Definitely all man.

Faith scuffed her slipper to alert him to her presence. She didn't want him thinking she spied on him. He glanced up then continued reading.

She gathered sandwich fillings on the counter. ''Can I make you a sandwich before we go?''

''Sure.''

Both struggled to maintain neutrality in their voices.

''Electric should be up soon. The worst of the storm passed.'' He glanced up suspiciously, suddenly realizing what she'd said. ''Before we go where?''

''Class.''

Nick's blank stare confronted her.

''As in, Lamaze Childbirth classes.'' She spoke slowly, enunciating each syllable. ''It was part of our prenuptial agreement. We marry. We don't fight over custody. You become my birth coach.''

Faith watched as the color seemed to drain from Nick's face. She peered closer, yup, there was a definite difference in his color. A bit of panic in his eyes, too. It served him right.

''Tonight? Isn't it early to be doing this?''

''Early? I'm less than a month from my due date. Anyway

you help the mares all the time. This'll be a cinch." She placed the sandwich in front of him. "Eat up. You're going to learn about birthing a baby tonight. The two-legged variety."

She noticed that he barely touched his sandwich. His appetite had vanished quicker than she could say *childbirth*.

Faith glanced at Nick. He maintained a stranglehold on the two pillows she'd told him they needed. The instructor and two other couples turned to look at them.

She offered her hand when the instructor approached. "Ms. Reynolds, I'm Faith Kincade…um…Harrison. We spoke on the phone."

"Sure." The woman pumped Faith's hand before turning to Nick. "This must be your husband."

He stepped forward. "Nick Harrison."

"I think we're all here. Let's get started. Faith if you'll sit with your back to your husband," Ms. Reynolds pointed toward the other couples. "Like the others. You'll need a pillow under your bottom."

Moments later, Nick tensed as Faith leaned back against him. She felt the hard muscles of his chest contract as their bodies met.

The instructor approached. "Mr. Harrison, you'll need to be off your knees. One leg outstretched on either side of your wife to support her." She walked back to the front of the room.

Two hours later, Faith's head pounded. It was torture. Pure, unimaginable torture. Her jaw ached from clenching her teeth together and the only thing that made it bearable was that Nick looked as tense as she felt. He appeared to be wound as tight as a new lariat.

They'd practiced breathing. Nick learned to stroke her back to relieve discomfort during labor. The real-life video had the other husbands groaning out loud. Nick only scowled.

She decided the delivery would be a breeze compared to the agony of sustained contact with Nick's body.

After a hasty goodbye to the group, Faith grabbed the pillows and escaped into the cool night air. She sucked great gulps of air. Aware of Nick standing behind her, she kept her gaze focused elsewhere.

"How many more?" Desperation laced his words.

"We're scheduled for three more." Her husky voice was barely audible. "We'll make it."

"Will we?"

Faith swallowed. "How hard can it be?"

Three weeks. Three more weeks until the baby was due.

Faith lay in bed the next morning and listened to the sounds of the ranch as it wakened. A rooster announced the rising sun. Down the hall, a shower turned on.

Nick.

She closed her eyes and tried to think about her previous year's tax forms for the store. It was a useless exercise. Nick was nearby, stark naked.

Soft, morning light would filter through the rough hair on his chest. The angles of his taut body shadowed and secretive. Skin slick to the touch.

That's it.

Faith forced the thoughts from her mind and glanced at the clock. One hour until Emily arrived.

The shower stopped. He'd be rubbing with a thick towel.

With a groan, she rolled toward the edge of the bed. Action was obviously the only thing to help her come to her senses.

Time to rise and shine and keep her mind out of Nick's bathroom.

She'd promised Emily they'd straighten the nursery and bake homemade cookies. Mab looked forward to a day in town on her own. Dressed, she headed for the kitchen. It was time to prepare for her pint-size friend.

Nick strolled in while she cooked the bacon. She sensed

his presence before he spoke, alerted by the nape tingle he inspired.

"Smells good." Nick rolled his shirtsleeves. Faith turned and stared at the dark hair scattered along his forearms. Her earlier shower fantasies popped into her mind. She looked at the amusement in his eyes. He seemed to know where her thoughts had wandered.

She turned back to the stove and focused on cracking eggs into the skillet. "Eggs and bacon this morning." *Brilliant conversation, state the obvious.*

"Any special plans today?"

"Emily's spending the morning with me." She scooped the eggs onto a platter with the crisp bacon.

"She likes you."

"It's mutual. I adore her." She sat across from him and spread her napkin.

Nick glanced pointedly toward the empty chairs on either side of him. He seemed to sense she'd chosen the far side of the table for refuge.

Tough. She didn't care what he thought.

"Have lunch with me?"

Faith managed to swallow her mouthful of eggs without choking. "Excuse me?"

"I thought we'd drive to some of the scenic places on the ranch." Nick studied his bacon rather than meeting her gaze.

She *did* want to see more of the ranch, so she tossed common sense to the wind. "What time?"

"Noon. We can take a picnic lunch. We'll see as much as possible before the afternoon thunderheads move in on us." He scraped the last bite from his plate and carried it to the sink. "Thanks for breakfast."

Settling a hat onto his dark hair, he slipped outside before Faith could utter an objection. She blinked as she watched his denim clad backside disappear from view. She didn't need to wander the ranch looking for a view, that one would do just fine.

*　　*　　*

Mab knocked as she put the last clean dish into the cabinet.

"Come in."

Emily waltzed in ahead of her mother with a ragged bunch of wildflowers gripped in her small hand. "Here, Miss Faith. Can we put these in the baby's room?"

"You bet." Accepting the bouquet, she placed it in a jar with water.

"I passed Nick on my way in." Mab's voice sounded curious. "He wanted to know if I'd be back by lunchtime."

Faith felt heat spread across her face. "He offered to show me more of the ranch."

Emily jumped from one foot to the other. "Me, too."

"No, honey. Miss Faith and Uncle Nick need time alone." Mab smiled at Faith.

"Are they gonna smooch like you and daddy?"

Faith felt her cheeks grow hotter. Innocent eyes looked up at her, as Emily waited for her answer.

Mab saved her. "Give Mommy a kiss. Now be good and help Miss Faith."

"Okay, Mommy."

Mab left.

Faith ruffled the child's curls. "Come on, munchkin. Let's get to work on the baby's room."

Singing, Emily skipped ahead and Faith followed. For the first time she allowed herself to wonder about the sex of the baby. Would it be a serious boy, like Steve? Or an effervescent girl, like Carrie?

Running her fingertips over her middle, she realized it didn't matter. It never had. As long as the baby was healthy, she'd be content.

Nick stopped the truck and stared at the back door of the house. The visit with his attorney had been strained. Putting a hold on all legal proceedings and halting the investigation was a risky step—a step his attorney advised against.

His palm scraped the rough whiskers on his jaw. Nick contemplated his reasoning. He was acting on the gut instinct that Faith held the key to what he needed to know. She destroyed his preconceptions about her more each day, contradicting his beliefs at every turn.

He'd planned the sightseeing to learn more, to ease information from her. Nick wished the trip were as simple as a drive in the country instead of being riddled with hidden motives.

Nick knew why he'd invited Faith, but he didn't understand why she'd accepted.

Shaking his head, he pushed the truck door open. He needed to get moving if they wanted to miss the afternoon lightning show.

Mab emerged through the back door with Emily in tow. Faith bent and hugged the child before handing Mab a plate heaped with cookies. Their laughter drifted across the yard.

Faith's smile twisted something inside him. Her face glowed and her sparkling eyes twinkled at Mab and Emily.

He walked toward them wishing that her smile was directed at him. Unguarded, Faith's eyes changed to a deeper blue. Gold flecks leapt from their depths when they focused on him.

Nick kicked himself internally, good and hard. The woman was trouble, more trouble than he needed in a wife or any other person. But convincing his libido was another matter.

"Hey, Nick." Mab greeted him. "Looks like we're off just in time."

"No need to rush."

"Uncle Nick, me and Miss Faith got everything ready for your baby." Emily grabbed his arm. "Wait till you see."

"I'll have to look later, squirt. After I take Faith for a ride." Nick directed Emily toward Mab. Emily's eyes were beginning to droop.

"Thanks again, Faith." Mab lifted the sleepy child. Emily wiggled and settled her head onto Mab's shoulder.

"Need me to carry her?" Nick offered.

"Oh, she's no heavier than a sack of groceries." Mab

smiled and strolled toward home. Emily peeked at them over her mother's shoulder and grinned.

"The rotten kid was faking?" He smiled and turned to Faith. "You ready?"

"All done. I hope you like chicken salad." She ducked into the kitchen and reappeared moments later with the picnic basket and a jacket.

A gingham cloth concealed the contents of the basket from Nick. He reached out to lift a corner, but she pulled the basket out of reach.

"You're worse than Emily." She hugged the basket to her chest. "Let's go."

He stared at the basket gripped against her body. He'd never wanted to be a basket before.

"The virtue of your lunch is safe. For now." Nick led the way to the truck. "I won't touch anything until you say it's time."

Faith's cheeks blazed with color at the innuendo in his words. He held the door for her, the picture of innocence. He noticed she placed the basket on the middle of the bench seat. A paltry barrier, but still a sign.

After fastening his seat belt, he turned the key and the engine roared to life. They passed beyond the old barn and headed west. The old wagon road was as good a place as any to start.

Sharp pine breezes blew in through the open windows. Faith looked around and appeared to relax, not hugging the passenger door so tightly. The truck bumped over the rutted track and they passed into the cool dimness of the sheltering pines.

When they struck a rut in the trail, Faith was jerked sideways. "A couple more jolts like that and you'll be delivering this baby on your leather seat."

He slowed the truck to a crawl and they drove for several miles in companionable silence.

He glanced at Faith to make sure she was enjoying the slower pace. "Do you hike?"

"Not recently, but, yes. I enjoy it." She cupped small hands on her stomach. "Carrie and I used to…" Her words trailed off before she faced the door.

"It's okay."

"What's okay?"

"Talking about your sister."

Faith faced him and searched his profile. "What about your brothers? Do you think of them? Do you wonder where Logan might be?"

No beating around the bush, she aimed straight at the heart of the matter and raised questions he didn't want to dwell on. He glanced at the openness in her eyes while she waited for an answer.

"Different situation." His tone was sharper than he'd intended.

"Different, how?"

"What was your family like while you were growing up?" He dodged.

Faith hesitated, drumming her fingers on the edge of the bench seat. "We were happy and close." She cleared her throat. "Carrie and I arrived long after Mom gave up trying to have children. She was forty when Carrie was born. I surprised them two years later."

"Mr. Burns mentioned your parents aren't alive anymore."

"Mom was diagnosed with cancer during my last year in college. She died six months later." She blinked rapidly.

He resisted the urge to touch her.

"Dad died in his sleep a year later. He never recovered from losing Mom. They were everything to each other."

Nick ground his teeth to keep from speaking. Commitment. A nice idea if you believed in fairy tales, but downright extinct as far as he was concerned.

"How about your family?" She managed to turn the microscope back on him and his so-called family.

"No one's spilled the Harrison story yet?" Sarcasm spiked his words.

"Mab offered a sketchy picture. I didn't mean to pry." She looked down at her hands.

He regretted spoiling the flow of conversation. Being defensive wouldn't encourage her to open up and trust him. It seemed twenty years hadn't eased the sting or the humiliation.

"Mom ran off when I was fourteen. She never looked back." Nick forced all emotion from his voice. "Steve and Logan took off as soon as they could. I stayed."

He interrupted Faith's murmur of sympathy. He didn't want nor need her pity. "Contact with Logan and Steve tapered off and eventually stopped. Dad died a year ago. Drank himself to death. The investigator I hired to find Logan after Steve died came up empty."

"I'm sorry."

The sincere, whispered words caused the muscles in his back to tighten. Nick didn't want this feeling of intimacy between them. Or the relief of confiding in another person. Especially Faith.

"Well, we're a sorry pair." Nick injected levity into his voice. It failed.

"We have the baby." Faith lay cool, soothing fingers against the skin of his arm. "And Logan is somewhere."

He looked at the pale fingers in stark contrast to his sun-darkened arm before glancing at the compassion in her eyes. Pulling his arm from under her hand, he slowed to a stop and shut the engine off.

Faith surveyed their surroundings. "Why did you stop?"

"Lunchtime. There's a trapping cabin in the trees. It's the first stop on the tour." He was determined to stay unemotional and uninvolved, acting merely as a tour guide.

Approaching Faith's door, he offered his hand to help her from the truck. Gripping his fingers, she slid off the seat. The friction of their skin sent his thoughts in dangerous directions. He released her hands and retrieved the basket.

"Where's the cabin?" Faith peered into the surrounding trees.

Nick pointed. "Through here."

After passing through the small grove of pines, they emerged in a small clearing. Slanting sunlight offered a softened view of the cabin set among the waving grass.

"It's lovely." Faith passed him and approached the cabin. "Can we go inside?"

"It's unlocked, code of the west. In case someone gets into a tough situation." He put the basket on the worn front steps and turned the knob. "You might want to stand back. Never know when an animal will take up housekeeping."

Faith jumped behind him and peeked over his shoulder. "Bears?"

He wanted to tease her and let her think it was a possibility. Instead he looked at her pale face and decided to reassure her. "Not likely. They wouldn't close the door."

Her shoulders sagged in relief.

"Of course, they are common in these parts." He couldn't resist the dig and grinned when he saw her glance into the trees.

She inched even closer. The wildflower scent clinging to her hair pulled at him, tantalizing and clean. Nick turned away and pushed the door open.

Scampering feet announced the presence of field mice. Dust swirled on the floor. Everything looked in place and undisturbed. No Harrison had entered the cabin in months, if not years. It was habitable only through Wayne's efforts. Nick shook the sullen memories from his head and relegated them into the past where they belonged.

"Looks fine." His terse words attracted Faith's attention.

"We can eat outside on the grass." She seemed to sense his dissension concerning the cabin.

"It just needs an airing." He lifted the brace bar from the shutters on the back window and swung them open on hinges that squeaked their protest.

Brilliant sunlight streamed in and illuminated the darkest corners of the room. A layer of dust coated the table beneath the window. The potbellied stove in the corner was stocked with wood. He watched Faith as she wandered to the small bookshelf. Her gaze turned to the bunks in the opposite corner. Her discomfort was a living thing—he could feel it growing from across the room.

Nick strode to the bed and thumped the thin mattress. A cloud of grime roiled into the air.

"Wayne airs the place out a couple of times a year. It's not used much." He tried to ease the apprehension from her eyes.

"Did you use it much in the past?"

"Years ago." Nick resisted the urge to tell her about the nights the Harrison brothers shared the old cabin. The past couldn't be resurrected.

Faith's attention turned from the bunks. But having her eyes fill with curiosity about him seemed worse.

Turning his back on her inquisitive gaze, he opened the final set of shutters. The two open windows allowed a cross breeze. The dank smell of neglect lessened, replaced, instead, with the fresh smell of pine and the sharp bite of mountain air. A heady combination.

Faith wiped the tabletop. Nick brought the basket in and they emptied the contents. Thick chicken salad sandwiches, moist grapes, and everything necessary to enjoy them littered the table.

Nick's stomach growled and he grinned when she jumped. "Relax. It's not a bear."

"Guess I'm not quite the outdoors woman I thought."

Seated across from her, he devoured the meal while Faith picked at hers. He noticed her flustered gaze returning to the bunk.

He chewed thoughtfully for a moment. "Faith?"

She jumped at the sound of his voice.

"You're safe."

"I know." She bit into a sandwich.

"Stop worrying about the bed. Nothing's going to happen."

His attempt at putting her at ease seemed to backfire. It

deepened the tension. Mentioning the bed was a rotten idea. His mind put thoughts into images that taunted his nether regions. He felt his jeans shrink a size.

Faith was eight months pregnant. She wasn't interested in a lustful romp. But, all he could think about were the creative things he'd like to try with her in the bunk.

"Tell me about the ranch." Her words sounded desperate—a ploy to divert his libido and her nerves.

Nick placed his empty water bottle next to his plate. Distraction was exactly what they needed.

Smart girl.

But the problem was she wasn't a girl. Faith was all woman *and* his wife. A soft, giving, responsive—he had to stop thinking along those lines. "It's been in the family for three generations." Nick rubbed his chin, focusing on the ranch and satisfying her curiosity.

"Granddad bought the parcel for next to nothing. He and Grandma built this cabin and lived in it for several years before building the original farmhouse. Wayne and Mab live in that now. Dad built the house I—we—live in."

"A lot of memories."

He frowned. "Yeah, not all of them worth remembering."

"But to live your entire life in one place. Work for one goal, the ranch. I can't imagine, but it sounds wonderful."

He studied the flush on her cheeks and liked the way her eyes lit up while she talked. "Where'd you grow up?"

"Several places. My folks were professors. So we lived on various university campuses." Faith quickly continued. "I'm not complaining. My parents were devoted to each other, and us."

Sensing there was more, Nick pressed. "But…"

"It was hard to…I don't know…form a connection to a place. Put down roots. I suppose that's why I envy you having the ranch." Her voice tapered off.

Nick was amazed. No one envied his upbringing. It seemed he and his family had been the object of pity for as long as he could remember.

Her words placed a new angle on the old situation. His mother had walked out, but he had the ranch. It was a part of him—it always had been.

Nick captured Faith's gaze. Words halted and her eyes widened, too large in her small face. The quick movement of her tongue across her dry lips destroyed his precarious control. He moved his hand to cover her trembling fingers.

He wanted, needed her hand to reach out and touch him. Let him know he wasn't alone with this hunger. The light touch sent his heart lurching against his ribs.

Darkness swept across the surface of the table. Absorbed in the private universe inside the cabin, Nick had failed to track the afternoon storms.

He shoved back from the table, toppling his chair. They needed to leave. Now.

"What's wrong?" She watched him with startled eyes.

"I'm as bad as a greenhorn. Letting the storm catch us." He leaned over the table and slammed the shutters. The bar dropped into place. "Rain will make the stream we crossed impassable."

Wind buffeted the cabin as if to emphasize his words. Faith leapt to her feet and hurried to close the remaining shutters seconds before rain pounded against the outer walls. With both windows covered, the interior of the cabin was cast in deep shadow.

Faith's back pressed against the door she'd slammed against the biting wind. "We can't leave, can we?"

"I should have paid better attention." Thunder punctuated his words—lightning flashed through the cracks around the shutters.

Stepping into the center of the cabin, she rubbed her arms. Nick turned to the stove and opened the door. Inside, shavings and kindling waited for the touch of a match. He turned to Faith.

"Wayne left us prepared. Any matches in that basket you packed or should I dig around in the cabinet?"

She rummaged through the basket, pulled out a lighter, and offered it to him.

The flame ignited the shavings and spread to the tinder dry kindling. Nick blew gently and coaxed the sparks to life. Orange flames leapt and crackled. He leaned back on his heels and adjusted the damper. "We'll have to keep our fingers crossed and hope a bird didn't nest in the stovepipe."

Minutes passed without smoke billowing into the cabin. Nick tossed two larger sticks into the consuming flames.

Golden. It was the only word Faith could conjure to describe Nick's profile highlighted in the glow of the fire. She watched him stoke the logs, mesmerized by the play of light in his tousled hair. Brown hair, alive with light, tumbled onto his forehead. Dancing shadows played across the line of his stubborn jaw and pulled her gaze to his lips, softened in the half-light. Faith wrenched her gaze away. She couldn't be here with him. It wreaked havoc on her tenuous peace of mind.

"Could we try to—" Ice balls slammed onto the roof and interrupted Faith's question. Hail. They'd have to wait it out.

Hovering near the stove, as far from Nick as possible without leaving the heat offered by the fire, she held her hands toward the warmth. The temperature had plummeted within minutes of the storm hitting.

Nick looked up, but she couldn't read his guarded expression. She wasn't sure she wanted to. Too many secrets were at risk. Not to mention her heart.

No! She refused to allow emotion to enter into what happened between the two of them. After Devon, she'd learned her lesson. The feelings she'd felt for her ex-fiancé were child's play compared to the emotions Nick evoked.

"You might as well get comfortable. Do you play checkers?"

His words surprised her. "Checkers?"

"The box is on the bookshelf. Has been for as long as I remember." Nick got up and crossed the room.

Faith watched the fabric tighten across his broad shoulders

when he reached for the box. She noticed the tapering toward his waist and feasted her gaze on the snug denim molded around his powerful thighs.

"Wanna play?"

She gaped at Nick. He'd read her mind. He knew she'd stood there drooling like a lovesick teenager.

He stared at her and repeated the question, the game in his hand. "You ready to play checkers?"

Of course.

His question had been innocent. It was only her obsessed mind twisting his words.

Faith moved to resume her seat at the table and tugged it closer to the heat and light emitting from the stove.

"Just try and stop me!"

CHAPTER ELEVEN

Nick watched Faith jump his last checker. Again. The woman had missed her calling. She could compete as a checker player in the Olympics. "Best two out of three?"

"You said that six games ago." She rearranged her pieces on the board.

"Give me a break. You trying to geld me?"

"No chance of that." Faith's hand froze over the board, as she seemed to realize what she'd said.

He enjoyed the tinge of pink resting on her cheekbones. She'd laughed often during the games. Conversation stayed on surface topics, safe topics. He checked his watch. "Three already. With the two hours of rain we've had, we'll need an ark to get back to the ranch."

She glanced up and smiled. "Stop trying to distract me. It's your move."

Studying the board, he planned his game strategy. "Where'd you learn to play so ruthlessly?"

"Dad taught me, but Steve honed my game."

Nick smoothed all emotion from his features, his skin pulled taut across his face. "Should've guessed. He always kicked my butt." He made his first move.

Hearing Steve's name cross her lips irritated him. Steve had been his brother and his childhood friend. Faith carried Steve's child. She'd obviously loved him. Probably still did. Nick hated competing with a memory. Why did he want to? He frowned at the top of her lowered head. He refused to envy his dead brother. It didn't make sense to be jealous when he hadn't even known her while Steve had been alive.

Faith chuckled while she double-jumped his game pieces. So much for staying focused on the game.

The legs of his chair scraped against the wooden floor planks as he stood. "I'll check the stream crossing."

"But we're in the middle of a game."

"Do you want to stay here all night?"

She stared at him with her brows drawn together.

Shrugging into his canvas jacket, he jammed his hat onto his head. "Keep the fire going."

Ignoring the bewilderment in her eyes, Nick slammed the door behind him. He paused on the porch and glared at the cloud-darkened sky before stepping into the downpour.

Spending the night with Faith wasn't an option.

He admitted defeat an hour later. They weren't going anywhere. Even if the rain halted now, the run-off ensured the stream would remain swollen through the night. What the hell were they going to do? They were adults—it shouldn't be too difficult to share the same sleeping space for one night. *Keep telling yourself that, buddy.* Realistically he knew it was going to be a long night.

Nick trudged toward the cabin, pausing at the edge of the clearing. Warm light beckoned from behind the shuttered windows. Twilight always descended early on stormy summer evenings.

Sloshing to the door, he shook the rain from his hat and coat before turning the knob. Coffee-scented warmth greeted him and tugged him, unresisting, inside.

Being alone in the isolated cabin increased Faith's fears. She worried that something had happened to Nick. What if he didn't come back?

Alphabetizing the books on the shelf hadn't consumed enough time so she'd turned to the single cupboard. Lighting the oil lamp she'd found, she rummaged through the shelves. A tin coffeepot and coffee distracted her from gloomy thoughts. Acquainting herself with the potbelly stove, she managed to stoke the fire and brew a pot of coffee. A can of chicken and dumplings warmed on top of the stove. All the comforts of home.

Except her room.

Faith flinched at the pounding outside the door. It matched the pounding of her heart. Pulling herself together, she pressed a hand to her chest to still the erratic beat. It was only the sound of boots on the porch, not a marauding bear.

Nick pushed the door open and stepped inside. He avoided her eyes while he removed his hat and coat. The slump of his shoulders told her what she wanted to know. And it wasn't good.

Pulling a chair next to the stove, he yanked a boot off. The sock underneath was soaked.

She gathered her courage and cleared her throat. "Any chance?" She hated the nervous tremor in her voice that revealed her apprehension.

He looked at her with the dripping boot dangling from his fingers. "We're not going anywhere." Dropping the boot, he leaned down to pull off the other. "I should have paid attention."

His self-blame helped her relax—he didn't seem to like the situation any more than she did. "It's my fault, too. I'm just grateful we have heat, food, and a dry place to stay." She turned to the stove and stirred the contents of the can.

Nick's second boot dropped to the floor.

"You're soaked. Use one of the bedrolls to wrap in and hang your clothes to dry."

Faith turned away and willed herself to ignore the rustle of clothing, the rasp of his pants zipper. She sensed the moment his strong fingers slipped the shirt off his shoulders. The squish of wet socks across the floor and a rustle of cloth alerted her to when he retrieved the blanket.

"Socks, too." She risked a glance over her shoulder.

He'd dragged his chair closer to the stove and stretched his hands toward the warmth. The blanket slipped from his shoulders.

Her stomach clenched into a tight ball of need. In the dim light of the lamp, Nick's skin gleamed. Warm and beckoning. While he stared into the flames, she stared at him.

No.

Faith forced herself to stare into the contents of the bubbling can. She refused to allow herself to think of Nick as a man. A sexy man. She tried to remember the reasons she hated him. They were valid reasons. What were they?

The time she'd spent at the Whispering Moon revealed the other side of the coin, Nick's human side. Some of the missing pieces in the Harrison family conundrum were coming together and she was forced to admit things were not black and white. Shades of gray clouded the issues.

"Smells good." His voice broke through her reverie.

"It's chicken and dumplings that I found in the cupboard with the coffee. Decaf, luckily." Caffeine had been chucked from her diet when the doctor confirmed her pregnancy.

He absently scratched his chest. "Remind me to restock supplies."

Faith silently cursed him for driving her mad by calling attention to his muscled body. She spooned the meal into tin bowls and poured coffee. Seated across from Nick at the small table, she deliberately focused on her food.

Why can't he wrap the blanket around his shoulders?

The drumming rain and crackle of the fire accompanied the meal. The intimacy of the scene curled around them until Faith felt the air thicken. If only she had the nerve to lean forward and touch the fullness of his lower lip that beckoned to her. Madness, hopefully temporary, but madness just the same.

Nick leaned back and the blanket slipped lower. "You can be in charge of the chuck wagon for fall roundup."

"Because I opened a can?" She looked at him over the rim of her cup. She hadn't planned ahead to autumn, instead choosing to take each day as it came. By fall the baby would be with them.

She reached for his empty bowl. "I'll get these things out of the way. Washing can wait till morning." She knew she was rambling. "I located the facilities while you were gone. It's a good thing we have flashlights."

Nick put his hand on her arm, halting her busy work. "I'm not going to attack you."

His tone soothed her raw nerve endings and reassured her of his intentions. But, Heaven help her, she wasn't sure about her own.

Giving a stiff nod, she reached for a flashlight and jacket. "Better make one last trip out tonight."

"I'll go with you."

"I'll be fine. Your clothes are probably still damp."

Nick reached to touch his discarded shirt. "Dry."

She spun away as the blanket slipped down the tanned length of his body.

He chuckled at her embarrassment. "It's not like you've never seen a naked man." A zipper's rasp accentuated his words. "You're pregnant."

Careful to keep her gaze focused on the wall, she drew a deep breath to calm herself. If he only knew how inexperienced she was.

"It's safe. You can look without compromising your maidenly virtue."

Nick lied. She realized it the moment she turned to face him. With his shirt unbuttoned, it was far from safe for her to look. Instead of feeling better because he'd covered some of his skin, she ached to push the fabric aside and gaze at all of him.

He reached for his socks, oblivious to her agitation. Her nipples tightened and pushed forward against her shirt. Quickly she shrugged into her jacket to hide her body's reaction to him.

After they were bundled up, he opened the door and aimed the flashlight beam into the deluge awaiting them outside.

Nick motioned to Faith. "Ladies first."

"Since when?" She hoped time in the cool rain would remove any romantic inclinations from her addled brain and fevered body.

She couldn't control her cringe when Nick touched her

elbow. Faith looked up at him, hoping he wouldn't guess the reason.

He halted her protest before it slipped past her lips. "I'm not taking any chances. Eight months pregnant isn't a good time to fall."

Mumbling under her breath, she allowed his hand to remain.

Nick adjusted his grip on Faith's arm. A rivulet of rain slipped inside his collar. The dash in the rain wasn't accomplishing what he'd hoped because his body's response to her was as strong as before.

Her obvious discomfort when his blanket had dropped stumped him. It nearly convinced him Faith was the innocent she appeared. One look at her profile proved otherwise. The woman was twenty-seven and pregnant—naked men were not a novelty.

Nick waited while she stepped into the outhouse. He tipped his Stetson forward and watched the water run onto the tips of his boots.

She emerged and held the door open. "Your turn."

"Let's get back." He didn't care if she noticed the gruffness in his voice. He wanted the night to be over. Instead, it was just beginning.

Moments later, he stomped into the cabin behind her. The walls seemed closer together. An unwanted intimacy seeped up through the rough-hewn planks of the floor, seeming to choke him. Hell, he hadn't even made it through a full hour without wanting to be intimate with her, how could he make it through the whole night?

Faith's features were clear in the glow from the fire. She tossed another log onto the flames and shook raindrops from her hair. Unknowingly the act was a sensual assault on his overstretched sex drive.

Nick turned to the bunk and yanked the top bedroll open. What was wrong with him? Where was his self-control? He couldn't come up with a good reason not to lure Faith to the bottom bunk and relieve some of the sexual tension choking the air from his lungs.

"I'll take the top." He avoided looking at Faith. "Adjust the flue to half and put the lantern out."

Pulling himself onto the thin mattress, he lay back and studied the timbers above his head. When the lantern flickered and went out, he knew he had a problem. The sound of Faith preparing the lower bunk and settling in was more effective than caffeine. Sleep was a long way off. He punched the pillow and tried to find a comfortable position.

He realized, too late, he should have forbidden lustful thoughts as a stipulation in the prenuptial contract.

As if that would have stopped them.

Faith willed her body to relax using every technique she remembered. Then, she made up some of her own. It was useless. With Nick above her...no, she wouldn't picture that scene.

Images rushed forward in her mind. Forbidden images of his body looming above hers, both of them coated with the sheen of perspiration from their shared passion. Faith groaned out loud.

"Are you all right?"

Mortified he'd heard her, she swallowed hard to remove the lump in her throat. Thank God, he couldn't read her thoughts. "I'm fine, just...stretching."

As far as lies went, it was feeble. She knew it, but hoped he'd buy it. Lying wasn't her style, but there was no way she'd share the fantasy that evoked the sound. Especially with the man who inspired it.

With her breathing suspended, Faith waited for Nick to question her flimsy explanation.

What am I doing? Why am I having sexual fantasies about my husband?

The man lumped her into the same category as his mother. Believed her to be one of the lowest forms of life. And, yet, she desired him. It wasn't fair.

A tear slipped out of the corner of her eye winding its way

into her hair. It wasn't possible. Somehow she'd fallen in love with her husband. A man who felt nothing more for her than contempt. And lust. It took her breath away. What if he discovered how she felt?

Frustrated by questions without answers, she rolled to face the wall. Trust is what it all came back to and what the whole situation hinged on. But what if she trusted Nick with the truth about the baby and he used it against her? She couldn't lose the baby, not even to him.

Faith stopped fighting the heaviness of her eyelids. Letting them close, she drifted toward sleep.

Sometime later, tantalizing aromas teased her awake. Faith raised lazy arms above her head and gave a catlike stretch. She smiled at the remnants of a salacious dream that lingered. Opening her eyes, she looked directly into the eyes of her carnal dream man. Cold reality whipped the smile from her lips.

Nick sipped a cup of coffee and stared at her. "The coffee's hot. Can I get you a cup?"

"Sounds good." She pushed upright and leaned against the log wall. Something seemed different. "It's stopped raining."

"A couple of hours ago. The stream should be navigable by noon."

"What time is it?"

"Nine-thirty, last time I checked."

"You're kidding." Sitting up in surprise, she nearly slammed her head against the upper bunk. "I can't remember the last time I slept this late."

He stood and poured a second cup of coffee. Faith accepted it and wrapped her hands around its warmth. The morning chill was held at bay by the potbelly stove and warm coffee.

She'd have to endure more time alone with him. How would she endure the sweet torture without revealing her newly discovered feelings? Each minute alone with him increased the danger—the danger to her heart. And pushed her closer to confiding in him.

She needed to get back to the ranch, distractions, people and reality.

Faith gasped when they rounded the bend. Yesterday's gentle stream rushed past, resembling a raging river now. She turned to Nick.

He spoke first. "It's not as bad as it looks. Only about a foot and a half in the middle." Shoving the truck into low gear, he continued. "The stream bed is rock, not sand. I've been through worse."

Knowing his explanations were meant to allay her fears didn't make them disappear. She still eyed the rushing waters with trepidation.

"Buckled in?"

"Yes," Faith whispered.

"Hang on."

The truck lurched forward at a steady crawl and eased into the water.

Faith released her death grip on the door handle with a soft sigh. "Whew, I thought it would be much wor—"

Midstream, the truck swayed. She strained toward Nick and away from the forceful water. Her hand reached blindly for reassurance and found a muscled thigh. She could feel his leg tighten beneath her fingers.

Nick stared ahead, still focused on the force of nature he tackled.

Faith held her breath until they emerged on the opposite bank. "You've crossed worse than *that?* Are you crazy?" She stared at him.

Adjusting the gears, he smiled at her. "Let's just say, I've tackled a few that would have had you wrapped around my neck instead of my leg."

Faith pulled her hand back. She'd forgotten to remove it. Heat rose in her face. Inching onto her side of the seat, she ignored Nick's laughter.

Nick congratulated himself on his handling of the situation. Not the stream crossing, but Faith's hand on his leg. The jolt of it still quickened his blood. He forced himself to concentrate on the mundane task of driving. Anything other than the picture in his mind of her stroking his naked thigh.

Lord have mercy.

Emerging from the trees, he pressed down on the gas. Nick wanted to escape the confines of the truck. He noticed a strange truck parked behind the house. At one time it had been blue. Now, rust seemed a more accurate description. It wasn't familiar.

"Who's that?" Faith leaned forward to peer through the windshield.

"Don't know." He pulled next to the neglected heap.

Nick approached Faith's door as she slid to the ground.

Her long legs didn't look like they were attached to a pregnant woman.

The back door squeaked and they turned toward the house. Nick's smile vanished when he recognized the man. Instead of the joy and relief he always expected to feel at this moment, he was filled with white-hot anger. Faith moved closer to him, seeming to sense his antagonism toward his brother who approached with an easy stride.

"You know him?"

"Yes." Nick ground the word through clenched teeth. He waited until the man met them in the middle of the yard and was within arm's reach. He slammed his fist into his brother's jaw and smiled thinly when Logan stumbled backward, caught off guard by the blow.

Faith's sharp intake of breath reminded him he had an audience.

"Maybe when you finish your macho display of stupidity, you could fill me in." Arms crossed low, she glared at him.

Glancing at the unkempt man who stood rubbing the discoloration spreading on his whiskered jaw, he decided it was time for introductions.

"Looks like the prodigal son returned." He impaled his brother with a look. "Faith, this is your brother-in-law."

"Logan?" Her eyes widened and she looked closely at the man. "Why'd you hit him?" Ignoring Nick's scowl, Faith approached Logan. The two eyed each other warily. Logan's sharp gaze took in her condition. She raised a hand toward the bruise inflicted by Nick, but stopped short of touching his face.

"Welcome home." Faith spoke in a whisper.

Nick flinched at the raw emotion in her voice. He stepped forward because he didn't like Logan's proximity to his wife, but refused to label the feeling as jealousy.

He confronted his brother. "Why *are* you here? Why now?"

Logan tipped his hat back. "One of your telegrams finally made it to me, a few months late. I assumed you expected me to show up." He pulled a much-folded telegram from a worn wallet. "I'll refresh your memory. *Dad dead. Stop. Steve dead. Stop. Steve's baby due in August. Stop.*" Logan replaced the telegram. "Sounds like a damned soap opera to me."

Faith broke the awkward silence following his words. "I'm sorry. That was a horrible way to hear bad news."

Nick ignored them both and stalked to the house. He couldn't explain the anger he felt toward his brother, even to himself.

"You must be…have been, Steve's wife."

Logan's words pulled Nick up short. He answered for Faith without turning. "She's *my* wife."

Logan motioned toward Faith's stomach. "So this is your—"

"No." Nick slammed the screen door. Let her explain the sordid details.

Faith prepared herself to face the disgust she'd see in Logan's eyes before turning. Looking into his expressive green gaze, she saw only curiosity. "It's a complicated story."

"Do I need to know the details?"

"No."

He glanced toward the ring on her finger. "Does it change the fact that I'll be an uncle?"

"I guess it doesn't." She smiled at the unusual man who stood before her. If only Nick were as accepting.

"You're in love with him." He looked toward the house.

She wasn't sure if it was a statement or a question. "I...well...circumstances...yes, I am." The final words were flung defiantly. She'd said it aloud and actually admitted her feelings to another person. Rather than feeling terrified, Faith felt the release of a burden. The relief of confiding in someone.

"Figured as much."

She was bewildered. "How?" If Logan knew, would Nick find out?

"The calf-eyed looks you threw his way. Even when you were spitting mad." He stared at her. "When are you going to tell him?"

"Probably never...it's not that easy." She didn't want Nick to have the power over her that would come if he didn't return her feelings. And she knew he didn't.

Logan granted a reprieve. "Any idea if I still have a room?" He pulled a duffel from the bed of the decrepit truck.

"The one next to Nick's old room?"

"Yes."

"It's still a bedroom." Faith cringed inwardly. She knew their sleeping arrangements would become common knowledge.

Logan trailed after her. They approached the stairs to Logan's room. She jumped when the door to the master bedroom swung open. Her bedroom.

Nick stepped into the hall. His expression remained unreadable as he spoke to Logan. "How long are you planning to stay?"

"As long as it takes." He stared back at Nick. "I'll see myself up, Faith."

She nodded because words refused to push past the dread

lodged in her throat. Faith watched Logan's back until he disappeared from view.

She turned to Nick. "He'll know we don't share a room."

"No."

"What do you mean, no?"

He pushed her bedroom door open with his boot and offered an unobstructed view. Nick's clothes lay in a haphazard heap on the bed.

"Oh." She glanced at him, and cleared her throat twice before she could speak. "I don't think so. Maybe he won't notice your room next to mine."

Nick narrowed his eyes. "And maybe he will. You'd rather march upstairs and explain our separate rooms to Logan?"

She drew a deep breath. He knew just where to hit. Their situation was private and she'd agreed to appear as a normal married couple to outsiders to set the stage for the baby's future.

"Where do you plan to sleep?" Faith held her breath.

"It's a big bed. We'll manage." His eyes sparkled.

The rat's enjoying this. "I can handle it if you can," she taunted. "It won't be forever."

"Why not?" Nick's mouth tugged upward at the edge.

She overlooked his deliberately provocative statement and pulled him into the room. Slamming the door, she faced Nick. "Any more wisecracks and you can sleep in the barn." Faith pushed the hair out of her eyes with a hand that trembled. "Let's put your things away."

She scooped an armload of clothing from the bed and found a pair of jeans and several pairs of briefs under her chin. Turning her gaze heavenward, she stalked to the dresser.

Nick chuckled.

"There's plenty of closet space and I'll clear a couple of drawers. You can put your things in." Faith felt Nick's gaze on her while she emptied a drawer. "This one should be big enough for your underthings and whatever you sleep in."

"You're standing on what I sleep in." He nodded at the briefs beneath her foot.

Faith jumped as if it were a rattler. He had to be joking or, maybe, he'd misunderstood. She'd offer him the benefit of the doubt.

"I meant your pajamas."

He nudged the briefs toward her with the point of his dusty boot. "That's it." Nick watched her and seemed to wait for a response.

"Find something else." She refused to budge on this point. No way she wanted to be bumping into his naked flesh in the middle of the night.

"I'm not changing a lifelong habit now." He didn't bother to hide his wide smile. "Stay on your side of the bed and you'll never know the difference."

Not know the difference? Was the man an idiot or did he truly believe what he said? Faith realized sharing a bed with a nearly nude Nick guaranteed little or no sleep.

She turned her back on his smiling face and emptied another drawer.

Dinner proved as comfortable as an infected tooth. The meal Faith prepared to perfection tasted like sawdust. She glanced through her lashes at the two men faced off across the dining room table.

Faith turned to Mab and saw her offer a small shrug. Wayne kept his eyes on his food while Emily chattered between each mouthful of food.

By inviting the Lees to dinner she'd hoped to relieve the tension. Instead they all stared at each other. Attempts at conversation dwindled and finally stopped.

Nick's frown had deepened at Wayne and Mab's exuberant welcome of Logan. What was wrong with the Harrison men? Pride was one thing, but this? Nick and Logan were behaving like emotionally stunted juveniles.

That's it. Faith slammed her fork onto the table just to break the cycle of moodiness between the brothers. All eyes focused on her and she turned to Mab. "Would you mind helping me with dessert?"

Relief flashed in Mab's eyes. "You bet." Both knew Faith didn't need help, but it beat the dinner atmosphere.

Pushing the swinging door with unnecessary force, she preceded Mab into the kitchen. Emily's oblivious prattle faded behind them as the door eased shut.

Mab sank into the nearest chair while Faith leaned her hip against the counter.

Mab snorted. "Tell me about the bruise Logan's sporting. If I know the Harrison boys, there's a story."

Faith lowered herself into the chair nearest her friend. "Just Nick's way of welcoming his brother home."

"Why am I not surprised?"

"I don't understand it. You'd think as the only family left, they'd pull together now."

"Not likely. There's a lot of hard feelings." Mab glanced toward the dining room. "On both sides."

"But, why? Their mother ran off over twenty years ago." She ran a hand over her stomach as the baby nudged.

"That was just the catalyst, honey. Mr. Harrison raised those boys with a hard sense of discipline and not much else. All three were expected to run the ranch. Together."

"And Steve and Logan left."

"Exactly. Nick stayed and carried the burden alone because he had no choice." Mab's voice lowered another notch. "He made this ranch what it is."

"But his father—"

"Was next to useless because he drank too much. It finally killed him. Thank God Nick finished his animal husbandry degree at night school before his father died. It took him six years what with having the responsibility of the ranch on top of it."

Faith now understood why he'd resented the child, the inheritance, even her. The ranch was his life. Now, Logan was back, perhaps to claim his share of what he hadn't helped build. Yes, she could understand Nick's bitterness. But she didn't have to like it.

Faith stood. "Better feed the bears and rescue Wayne." She pulled the towel off the blueberry cobbler.

Mab carried the ice cream from the freezer.

After the bowls were filled, Faith turned to leave the room, but Mab stopped her with a gentle hand on her arm. Faith looked back and raised her eyebrows.

"When are you going to tell him?"

Faith felt an icy hand squeeze her heart. She schooled her features to reveal nothing. "What?"

"The truth."

Remaining silent rather than heaping lie upon lie, she carefully placed the heavy tray on the counter. Her trembling hands had threatened to spill its contents.

Mab met her gaze and smiled kindly. "About the baby and Steve. I've only known you a few weeks, but I'd swear you aren't capable of betraying your sister. I don't understand what's going on, but I know you're a decent person."

Moisture built behind Faith's eyelids. Mab's unconditional support was an unexpected treasure.

"I'm not asking for your secrets, Faith. I just want you to know you can count on me."

Faith reached out and hugged her friend as the tears slipped over her lashes. Someone believed in her without explanations or facts. She welcomed the support offered, but one thought gnawed at the edge of her happiness.

Why wasn't it Nick?

CHAPTER TWELVE

A WEEK slipped by as Faith watched Logan's attempts to help with daily operations around the ranch. And she observed as Nick gradually accepted his brother's help. Mealtimes weren't a warm, cozy affair, but at least the men talked now.

Logan reluctantly revealed facts about how he'd spent the years since his exodus from the Whispering Moon. A stint with the Air Force in the volatile Middle East was mentioned, but not his mission. His mouth clamped closed if it was mentioned.

Rodeo had spurred him to keep moving and gave meaning to his days.

Nick pushed for answers. "Don't you keep a permanent post office box somewhere?" They were fortunate the telegram found him at all.

"Hell, no." Logan glanced at Faith. "Sorry, ma'am. I bunk with one of the other riders or, depending on the town, a...friend."

She watched the redness creep up his neck and marveled that a man who'd experienced so much of the world could still blush.

Later that day, Faith took a walk to the corral, and found Nick speaking softly to the new mare that had arrived the night before. The poor thing had been adopted out after the county discovered her owner wasn't treating her humanely. Nick's large hand ran down the mare's neck as she rolled her eyes back, fearful of the hand she couldn't see.

Nick walked several feet from the mare and held his hand out. He had to gain her trust. It's what had to be established before the mare would feel safe again and begin to heal emotionally.

The mare had to trust that the hand offered wouldn't harm her. Or disappoint her. Faith understood, perhaps too well.

Resting her chin on the top rail of the fence she shielded her eyes from the bright sun and absorbed each detail of Nick's broad back. There was no harm in looking. Only in touching.

Ha!

Six nights they'd shared a bed. Six of the longest nights of her life. Nick would wait until she turned the light off before entering the room. For six agonizing nights Faith had listened to the scrape of his zipper in the darkness and held her breath as discarded clothing slipped to the floor.

She always imagined him towering over her in the dark, magnificent and only inches from the bed. She tried to keep her breathing deep and steady when his weight eased onto the mattress. Each night was agony. Pure, sweet agony.

Nick's breathing would even out almost instantly as he slipped into untroubled sleep. But hours usually passed before her fevered longings allowed her to doze into fitful sleep.

Faith rubbed her weary eyes and blinked her inner fantasies away. Peaceful sleep was a distant memory. Avoiding contact with Nick's exposed flesh left her stiff and disagreeable in the morning. Imagine.

Logan slipped up next to her and rested a boot on the bottom rail. "He's got a way with them."

"With who?"

"Skittish mares."

She followed his gaze to where Nick still worked with the mare. "Yes, he does."

The mare approached Nick with nostrils flared, still uncertain. Faith thrilled at the tentative steps. Neck outstretched, the mare sniffed the sugar cube offered in his palm. She nuzzled the treat before finally accepting it.

Nick turned to look at Faith. She smiled at him, sharing

in the small triumph. He returned her smile before breaking the tenuous connection and returning his focus to the horse.

"You left your mail on the table."

Logan's voice startled her. She'd been so absorbed in one brother that she'd forgotten the other stood near. "I'll clear it later. Hope it wasn't in your way." Faith's attention remained on the pair in the ring.

"There was an open statement in the stack. I didn't realize it was yours until too late."

She felt her smile slip and swallowed as dread rose in her throat.

"The wind blew everything on the floor. I didn't mean to nose in your business." He hesitated. "The letterhead caught my eye."

How could I be so careless?

Because like a girl with her first crush, Faith wanted to skip out here and ogle her husband.

"Is there something you want to say?" Only the slight quaver in her voice revealed her disquiet. Faith forced herself to meet Logan's questioning gaze.

"Why are you getting a bill from a fertility clinic?"

Faith swung to look at the mountains in the distance and considered her options. A cloud passed in front of the sun as she looked for a way out of the situation. What story should she tell? Lies were compounding on top of lies, till the heap of them seemed bigger than the surrounding range.

Closing her eyes, she made her decision. She wouldn't lie to Logan. They had formed a tenuous bond and she wouldn't jeopardize it.

"Just tell me it's none of my business." Logan looked to where Nick led the mare by the halter. "Will you answer one question?"

"If I can."

"Does Nick know about the clinic?"

Faith stared into his eyes, trying to read his expression. "No."

"Why?"

There was no way to put it all into words.

He tried again. "Why, Faith?"

"Because I'm terrified." She stiffened when his arm encircled her shoulders.

"Of what?"

Faith answered honestly. "Losing it."

"The baby or your marriage?"

"Yes." Faith locked her gaze with Logan's and willed him to understand what she had no words for.

Nick eased the saddle blanket onto the mare's back. She stiffened, but accepted it. It was a small step, but she was learning to trust him. Turning to share the small victory with Faith, he felt the air rush from his lungs.

She and Logan stood close together. With their heads bowed and close together, they appeared deep in conversation. Logan's arm circled Faith's slight shoulders. Nick was slammed in the midsection by overwhelming possessiveness. Why was Logan touching his wife? And why was she letting him?

Six nights Nick had endured hell on earth. Faith's scent tortured him all night and reminded him that he needed to move only inches to touch her. He'd resisted. Working late into the night so he'd be exhausted when he fell into bed and be able to resist his baser urges.

Now, there she stood allowing another man to touch her. Nick decided it was past time to stake a husband's claim. He released the mare with a gentle pat and pulled the blanket from her back.

Making his way to the fence, he swung over the rails. Neither of them looked his way. What were they talking about?

"Hello, Wife." Nick halted directly behind Faith. The two jumped apart.

Nick clenched his hands into fists. Logan stepped away. Faith stared up at him. Nick didn't like the apprehension mirrored in her eyes. "Miss me?"

Confusion crept into her gaze. "I wanted to see how the mare—"

He pulled her against his chest and halted her words with his mouth. What started as a punishment, changed into pure pleasure. Faith's startled gasp was muffled against his lips and he took advantage of her confusion to plunge his tongue into the sweetness of her mouth.

Allowing the frustration of the past nights to override his common sense, he tasted and teased until everything faded and he couldn't remember why he'd started this. He concentrated instead on the change in Faith's response.

Tentatively, then more boldly, her tongue tangled with his. He felt his control slip. The arms that lifted and encircled his neck ensured it. He shoved his hands under the back edge of her shirt and roamed his hands over the silken skin of her back.

Faith moaned and molded her curves to his throbbing body. Nick removed his hands from her back and grasped her shoulders to push her back a step. Dazed eyes looked up at him, lids heavy with unquenched desire. Her swollen lips tempted him to take more.

"No." He ignored her startled gaze and stalked to the house. He needed a cold shower and a stiff drink. In that order.

Logan had vanished.

Faith watched Nick leave. She suffered the sting of his rejection, the second one. The screen door slammed as he vanished into the house.

Faith brushed her lips with her fingertips where they still burned from the contact with his mouth. It was insanity. She wanted so much more. Needed so much more. Why this man?

The kitchen. Nick was in the kitchen. *God, no.* Racing as quickly as possible, Faith prayed she wasn't too late. Gasping for breath, she yanked the door open and stepped into the dimness of the kitchen.

It was too late.

Nick glared at her with disbelief etched on his features. He clutched the bill from the clinic in his fist.

"Is this what you were after?" He brandished the paper in the air. "Careless of you, don't you think?"

Faith approached cautiously and stopped within arm's reach of him.

He scanned the paper. "Monthly HCG injections, and three separate oral medications. And the most expensive charges for egg retrieval from Carrie Kincade."

She felt moisture bead her upper lip and closed her eyes. Nauseated didn't begin to describe her physical reaction to the nightmare situation.

"I'm no expert, but this doesn't seem to indicate an old-fashioned, natural pregnancy. Look at me, Faith. I want to see your eyes while you lie your way out of this."

It was difficult to face his anger without flinching, but she was determined to hide her fear.

"The final charge for in vitro fertilization and implantation of an embryo." Nick's face darkened. "Would you like to share the details of what I'm reading?" He waved the paper under her nose.

Incensed, she snatched the paper from his fingers and faced him defiantly. It was time for the truth. "What it means, Mr. Harrison, is that I am a partial surrogate."

"A what?"

"Carrie's eggs were fertilized by her husband's sperm in a petri dish. Three of the most viable embryos were then implanted into my womb. One survived." Faith folded the sheet in half and smoothed the crease. "Not conventional, but still a miracle."

Nick folded his muscled arms across his chest. Distant and implacable. "Why?"

"Carrie wasn't able to sustain a pregnancy. She suffered through three miscarriages. It was destroying both of them."

She moved to the window overlooking the backyard. How could everything look so normal? The sun filtered through the aspen branches. Birds gathered bugs for lunch. Was it only her world terribly out of sync?

"Did you sleep with Steve?" Nick's voice was strained and cold.

Faith faced her accuser, her husband. "No! I loved Steve like a brother. He and Carrie were my family." Her voice broke and she drew a shuddering breath.

"Why did you let me believe you betrayed your sister?"

"You didn't know me, would you have believed any denial I made?" She saw the answer in his expression.

His eyes narrowed. "It was the baby. You thought I'd fight harder for custody if I realized we were on equal footing with our claims. If I found out you were just the surrogate."

Faith didn't deny it. It was true and they both knew it. "Just a surrogate?" Her chin shot up. "This baby couldn't be more mine than if I'd conceived it. It's me who feels it move. Me, who has the privilege of nourishing it through my body."

"But you didn't conceive it. God, I'm a fool." Nick shoved his fingers into his hair, knocking his hat to the floor. "No wonder you jumped at the marriage offer. It made you feel safe."

"Nothing is more important to me than this child." Her heart was breaking and drifting to the floor in tiny shards of hope.

"Enjoy it while you can because as soon as the baby arrives I'll request an annulment. Then I'll obtain sole custody." He scooped his hat from the floor without meeting her gaze. "Things are looking up for my case."

Faith reached out and touched his arm. "Nick, please. We have to think of the baby. Not our pride." She hated feeling as though she was begging, but felt everything slipping away, her hope for a stable future for the baby. And her secret dreams of a relationship with Nick.

He yanked his arm from her hand as though he couldn't stand her touch. "Save it for the judge." He strode out of the house, slamming the door.

Faith stood in the middle of the empty room and willed herself to waken from the nightmare. Ruefully she headed to her room with the damaging paper gripped in cold fingers. The only one who could save her from the nightmare was herself. It was time to make use of her backbone.

Faith needed to get away from the ranch and from Nick. She needed familiar scenery and yearned for time to pull herself together and decide on a course of action. Time to lick her wounds and get on with life.

Twenty minutes later, she penned a brief note to Nick. Her packed suitcase waited at her feet. She'd called Mab and explained that she needed to tend to business at the bookstore. It wasn't a lie. She'd neglected the store. A personal visit *was* overdue. It was a weak excuse. Nick would see it for what it was. A frantic stampede as far from him as she could manage.

Laura would be back in her own apartment by now, so Faith would have the house to herself. Things had fallen into place.

The farmhouse dwindled to a speck in her rearview mirror. Moments later, it completely vanished from view.

Nick shouldered the last of the fifty-pound grain sacks and hoisted it atop the others stacked against the barn wall. An hour of honest-to-God, hard work diminished the bulk of his rage. He'd admitted to himself that most of his anger stemmed from his damaged ego.

He'd believed that he and Faith were growing closer. She had seemed more open and trusting. So, why hadn't she trusted him enough to confide the truth of the baby's conception?

A snort from a nearby stall was his only answer. Nick stepped into the midafternoon sun.

Logan marched at him and stopped only inches from Nick's face. "What did you do to her?"

"What the hell are you talking about?" He wasn't in the mood for riddles.

Logan shoved a piece of notepaper at him and Nick scanned the stilted words. Damn the woman, Faith was gone. Supposedly to catch up on store business. She hadn't stayed long enough to sort things out. Remembering his harsh words, he couldn't blame her.

"I'm only going to ask one more time, then I'm going to kick you from here to the barn. What did you do to her?"

"It's none of your business." *I acted like a raging bull.*

His brother refused to back down. "I'm making it my business."

"She's *my* wife."

Logan smiled sardonically. "Is she?" He shook his head. "You saw the statement from the clinic?"

Nick didn't bother to answer. They both knew he had.

"Didn't you think about offering her the benefit of the doubt?"

"She didn't deny anything."

"I can't imagine why not. When you get an idea in your thick skull, there's no shaking it loose." Logan turned and walked two paces. He spoke again without looking at Nick. "You're going to drive her away. And you don't have a clue what you'll be throwing out."

Was he throwing something away? Faith didn't want to be married to him, did she?

Logan walked away.

Nick scanned the note again and tried to read between the lines of clipped words. Gone to check on store, what did that mean? What if she wasn't planning to return to the ranch?

Without stopping to consider the consequences, Nick hurried to the house. He needed to shower and pack. Faith was coming home with him. He'd accept no other option.

By the time he was ready to leave it was near dinnertime. Nick needed to get on the road for the three-hour drive that lay ahead—too much time had passed since Faith had left. He tossed an overnight bag into the cab of the truck.

Where the hell am I going?

Nick had no idea where Faith's house was located. How

would he find her once he arrived? Ten minutes later he found the address on a crumpled paper in her room.

Nick cranked the engine. Putting the truck into gear he spotted Logan aiming a jaunty salute as his send-off. A wish for good luck, perhaps? God knew he needed it.

Faith parked in front of her house. She couldn't think of it as home any longer. The ranch now claimed that distinction. Weary feet carried her to the front door and stale air poured out as she entered. It didn't even smell like home.

Get over it, this is your real life, remember?

Home it would have to be. At least for the next few days, until she could figure out what to do. Faith kicked the door closed and carried her small bag into the bedroom. At the moment a hot shower sounded like the closest thing to heaven. The two hours on her feet at the store had felt like days.

She stepped under the relaxing spray and stayed until the hot water was gone. Pruney, but refreshed, she stepped out of the shower stall. Faith shrugged into her silk robe and rubbed her hair with a towel.

She padded to the kitchen and prepared a soothing cup of tea. Inhaling the gentle aroma, Faith willed herself to relax. She was fine. Things were complicated, but she'd get through it. There was no choice. The baby needed her.

Walking into the dark living room, she turned on a small reading lamp and welcomed its beacon in the twilight as she absorbed the soft light it offered.

Lowering herself onto the couch, Faith laid her head back and let her eyelids drift down. Thoughts she'd suppressed since the confrontation with Nick rushed to the surface. The ugly words and accusations seemed to belong to another life, another person. But, unfortunately, they didn't.

He had every right to be angry, to mistrust her. But she honestly didn't know if she'd do anything differently. She'd made the best decisions possible with the information available. Now, Faith didn't know what the next step was.

She stared into the wisps of steam drifting from her cup. Hoping to locate an answer in the amber liquid.

"Yeah, right." Her mumbled words sounded overly loud in the quiet house. The tea held no power to help her. She'd have to help herself.

The doorbell chimed. She glared toward the door. Who in the world knew she was here?

Faith tightened her sash and flipped the porch light on. Pushing the drapes back, she rolled her eyes heavenward. *Not him, not tonight.*

Turning the dead bolt, she opened the door. "What do you want?"

"Now, is that any way to greet your fiancé?"

"Ex-fiancé."

Devon pushed the door wider and staggered inside. Faith smelled the stench of alcohol and stale cigarette smoke clinging to his jacket when he brushed past her. She had to get him out of the house—she definitely didn't want to deal with a drunk tonight. Especially *this* particular drunk.

He leaned toward her. "How 'bout a kiss? Or are you still the village prude?" He shuffled closer.

"I'd like you to leave." She averted her face to avoid the stench of his alcohol-warmed breath. "I'm married."

"Ha." He belligerently walked to the couch and collapsed onto the cushions.

Leaving the front door open as an avenue of escape if needed, she crossed her arms protectively over the baby. The gesture drew Devon's bloodshot stare.

"You giving that husband of yours what you wouldn't give me?" Devon leered at her. "Rebound relationships never work."

Faith couldn't believe she'd been engaged to this lump of humanity masquerading as a man. Thank heaven she'd never slept with him, much less married him.

But, she was curious. "How did you know I'd be here?"

"Small town. People talk. 'Specially when you waltz into town hugely pregnant." He glared at the evidence of her pregnancy. "Most people who saw you assumed the brat was mine."

Faith flinched. She'd never considered that possibility.

Devon rambled. "If they only knew." He stood and stumbled toward her. "The virgin ice queen never gave it up to the guy she was supposed to marry."

She reached out for the nearest thing she could find. The weight of a crystal clock chilled her hand. She didn't think Devon would physically harm her, but he was no longer someone she knew. His ego was hurt, certainly not his heart. He'd shown his lack of feelings for her by abandoning her because she'd offered to carry this baby. His shallow thoughts were only for himself.

Devon grabbed for her.

Faith nearly jumped out of her skin when strong hands pulled her out of his reach. Heart racing, she glanced at her rescuer. Nick. His strong hands gripped her shoulders. It didn't matter how he happened to be here when she needed him, she was simply grateful. She allowed her tense body to relax against the solid strength of his chest.

Devon squinted at them. He focused on Nick. "Who the hell are you? This is private."

"That's right." Nick's calm voice was in stark contrast to the muscles bunched under his jacket. "My *wife* and I would like some privacy."

Devon's face reflected his conflicting emotions as he considered challenging Nick. Finally, resignation settled on his pasty features.

"I'll be back, it's not finished yet." Devon stumbled to the door.

"I suggest you forget this address." Nick's words caused him to pale further. "We don't want to see you again." He searched Faith's eyes for confirmation.

She nodded.

Devon slammed the door and Faith listened to him stumble down the porch steps, his muffled curses slurred. She moved past Nick to peer out the window.

"We can't let him get behind the wheel."

Nick dangled a set of car keys from his fingers. "He won't. I took his keys out of the ignition after I watched him weave up the sidewalk."

She concentrated on the keys because she couldn't meet his gaze. If he'd seen Devon approach the house then Nick must have heard everything. She tried to recall what Devon had said.

Louder curses and the slam of a car door echoed in the night. She turned to the window and watched Devon kick his car tire before he stomped off.

"You're a coward." Nick's soft voice was too close. "Why'd you turn tail and run?"

"How did you find me? Why did you find me? The note told you I'd be back."

"Was he telling the truth?" He watched her face.

Faith didn't need to ask whom. "Which part?"

"The virgin queen part."

She found Nick's gaze fixed on her face. "Faith, I owe you an apology for this morning."

She shuffled uncomfortably and looked at the carpet, but his hand beneath her chin forced her to meet his eyes.

"Things were out of control. I still don't know what's going on." It was his turn to look uncomfortable. "Let's concentrate on the baby here." He placed his hand on her belly. "We'll worry about the rest later."

A flicker of hope flared in her heart, but she pushed it down. How much of his apology was for her? And how much was concern about her stress levels? The baby's health?

Whispering a hurried good-night, she quietly closed the door behind her. Rather than easing her frenzied thoughts, Nick's apology had contributed to the muddle.

Faith turned to the kitchen. She needed a warm glass of milk. Sleep was a universe away.

Morning arrived early. Or so it seemed to Faith. Sleep had eluded her until the early hours. She rubbed the taut skin of her stomach and the baby nudged back. Reassured, she sat up and swung her feet to the floor. A wave of dizziness washed over her.

Take it slow. Her lack of sleep over the past week was catching up.

She could hear Nick banging around in the kitchen.

Faith dressed after a quick shower. She entered the kitchen in time to watch Nick bang his head on the corner of a cabinet door he'd left open.

"Damn thing." Nick slammed the vicious door.

Faith giggled and he turned to glare at her.

Faith raised her eyebrows at the sight of the pink gingham apron tied around his waist. "Sorry. Must be the sight of your lovely apron."

"Keep laughing and you can make breakfast." Nick said with a smirk as he waved a spatula in her face.

"No laughs from me." She poured a glass of juice. "How's your head?"

"I think my ego sustained more damage than my head." Nick turned back to the skillet. "How do you want your eggs?"

"I think I'll pass. My stomach isn't feeling great this morning." Faith kept her voice casual so he wouldn't make a big deal out of nothing. "I'll just stick with toast."

"No wonder you're such a tiny thing." Nick looked at her. "How long until the due date?"

"Still about three weeks away."

"Is this too early for something to happen?"

"Not really." She drained her glass, aware of Nick's attention. "Stop looking panicked, nothing's happening." She dismissed the twinges she'd experienced from her mind. If he knew about them, he'd just insist on rushing her to the nearest hospital.

"I'll follow you to the ranch. Do you need to stop at the bookstore before we head back home?"

Faith relished the feelings that surfaced when he mentioned home. It was true. Over the past months the

Whispering Moon had become home. Nick's presence made it that, even if he didn't realize it. Just seeing him every day and hearing his voice made it home. She finally understood what Carrie had felt for Steve. Unfortunately, Nick didn't feel about her the way Steve had felt about his wife.

"Faith?"

She pulled herself back to real life. "I'm sorry, yes, I need to run by. But, you don't need to wait for me."

"Humor me, it's a man thing." He set a plate of toast on the table.

Faith lifted the top piece. "Okay."

Thirty minutes later, Faith locked the front door. A glance in her rearview mirror confirmed Nick was behind her. She parked in front of the store and waved to him before she stepped inside.

Laura stood behind the counter. "Hey, girl. I didn't expect you this morning."

"I thought I would take some books back for Emily."

"Are you feeling all right?"

"Of course, why?" She was surprised by the question.

Laura came around the counter. "You look pale. Sure you're okay?"

"Yes, Mother, I'm sure."

"Do you want me to drive you back?"

Faith stammered. "Nick's going to follow me there."

"He's here?" Her friend's curious gaze swept the sidewalk in front of the store. "Which one is he? When did he arrive? Why did he come?"

Faith laughed. "Yes. In the truck. Last night. Looking for me." She strolled to the children's book section. Laura walked to the window and pressed her face against the glass.

"Oh, my, he's gorgeous." She turned accusing eyes to Faith. "You didn't tell me he was drool-worthy."

Faith's head tilted thoughtfully. "I guess he is." Laura was the only person she'd confided in about the details of the marriage she'd entered.

"You're in love with him, aren't you? Don't even try to

deny it. Is he going to break your heart?'' Laura approached her.

"I can't recall if my heart consulted me beforehand.''

After selecting two books, she headed to the counter. A book on Colorado's Native American heritage caught her eye and before she could change her mind, she picked it up for Nick. She'd noticed several similar books around the ranch and knew he'd enjoy it.

Logging the books into the computer, she tucked them into a bag.

A frown tugged at Laura's lips. "Call if you need me. I'll show up like the cavalry.''

Faith hugged her quirky friend. "Thanks. I'll call soon.''

"You better.''

The bell above the door rang as she stepped into the warm sunshine. Tossing her bag onto the passenger seat, she looked back at the store. Laura stood at the window, arms across her chest. Her stance protective and threatening.

Faith merged into traffic and checked Nick in her mirror. The miles to the ranch, to home, melted away.

Home. But for how long?

CHAPTER THIRTEEN

DURING the trip, the gentle twinges gradually altered. An hour from the ranch, sharp pain knifed across her midsection. Faith jerked the wheel before her grip steadied, hoping Nick hadn't noticed.

No such luck.

Nick flicked his lights at her. A highway sign stated a rest area only two miles ahead. She pointed the sign out to him, deciding two miles was soon enough to pull over.

As the exit came into view, another pain caused her to yank the wheel to the right. Nick leaned on his horn. Faith ignored him and concentrated on finding a parking place while she breathed through the contraction.

Contractions. Oh, Lord, what else could they be?

Nick appeared at her window. "What's wrong with your car?"

Faith looked at him and wondered why his voice seemed to come through thick cotton. She saw comprehension in his eyes. He yanked the door open and crouched next to her as she let her eyelids close.

"When did it start?"

Faith forced her eyes open to reassure him. "I'm okay. Sorry I scared you. It's probably just Braxton Hicks."

Nick reached out and smoothed the hair from her damp forehead. "Braxton, who?"

"False labor."

"Labor!" His voice rose. "How can you know if it's real or not?"

"I guess I can't." Faith felt light-headed. "I can't remember exactly what the book said."

She grabbed Nick's hand when another pain seized her. She heard him speaking, but didn't understand the words.

176

Focusing inward, she breathed through the discomfort. When the contraction finally subsided she stared at Nick. He looked as pale as she felt.

"These don't feel false."

"How close are they?"

"I'm not sure. Four, maybe, five minutes." She mumbled.

Leaning into the car, he placed an arm under her legs and the other behind her back.

"What are you doing? I can walk."

Nick lifted her gently from the seat. "I'm putting you in the truck. There's no way you're driving." He tightened his arms around her.

"Don't be ridiculous. I'm certain it's not—" She tensed as another contraction robbed her of breath.

He stopped walking and pulled her against his chest. "Breathe, that's it."

Faith focused on his soothing voice as Nick moved and placed her on the seat of his truck.

"Nick?"

"What?" His voice was strained and brusque.

"My things." She saw impatience flare in his eyes. "Please."

He stalked to the car and grabbed her suitcase and purse. After locking the car, he jumped into the driver's seat of the truck.

"Move over here."

She hesitated.

"I need to know when you're having contractions. And you're just stubborn enough to keep it from me." Nick waited for her to slide over then slammed the truck in gear and roared out of the lot.

The press of his arm against her shoulder reassured her. Faith was scared and needed the comfort of his body next to hers.

"This reminds me of our wedding day." His voice flowed over her. "You were in the middle then, too."

"That'll happen when you buy a truck with a bench seat."

She offered a strained smile. "One woman or another will try to sit in your lap."

"Seems like we're always pulling up to the emergency room in this old truck." Nick played along with the distracting prattle.

"Let's see how fast we can make it this time." Her words trailed off as she gripped the edge of the seat and rode another contraction.

Nick pressed the accelerator to the floor. The miles rushed past, but it seemed like slow motion.

Each time Faith suffered silently through a contraction, he cursed his helplessness. Knowing there was no way to help filled him with demoralizing rage and an overwhelming sense of protectiveness toward her.

Nick phoned the hospital on his portable phone and prepared them for Faith's arrival. Then he called Mab. Her calm voice lowered the panic building inside him like a coiled rope. She insisted on meeting them at the hospital and he didn't argue.

Twenty minutes later, he raced into the hospital lot. Ignoring the directional signs he stopped in front of the emergency entrance. Nick reached over to unhook Faith's seat belt.

"Oh!" She looked stunned. "That was different."

"What?" Nick tensed and prepared to run inside for a doctor.

She wouldn't meet his eyes. "I'm sorry. I think my water broke on your seat."

They bumped heads looking down. Both were silent.

He spoke first. "Should it be that color?"

Faith's terrified eyes gave him the answer. Brownish-red was not the right color.

"Nick..." Panic edged her voice.

He had to keep her calm. "It's okay. We're at the hospital. Put your arms around my neck." Nick shook her shoulder when she didn't respond. "Faith?"

She remained still, her lashes dark smudges against colorless cheeks. Nick swept her up and hurried to the door. Several people in hospital garb met them with a gurney.

"Mr. Harrison?"

"Yes." Nick placed Faith on the white-sheeted bed. They immediately rolled her inside.

"Sir, we'll need you to fill out some forms and update us on your wife's condition." A matronly nurse kept pace with him as he jogged beside the gurney.

Dr. Grant waited inside. He directed the attendants into a private exam room. After he pulled the door closed, the doctor checked Faith's pupils and pulse as a nurse began undressing her. Nick hovered near the head of the bed, uncertain where to look or what to do. Helplessness did not suit him.

"How long has she been unconscious?" The doctor questioned him while the nurse finished undressing Faith beneath a sheet.

"Three or four minutes." He stared at Faith's small face against the stark white of the pillow. "She said her water broke. We noticed the color and she passed out."

Dr. Grant looked at him with a penetrating stare. "You're aware of the risks involved with this pregnancy?"

"Yes. Is she all right?" Nick wanted answers. Now.

"We'll have to wait for a couple of lab readings on the amniotic fluid." He turned to the nurse monitoring Faith's vital signs. "I'll need a transfusion cart if it turns out to be blood in the fluid. Two pints to start. Let's get a fetal monitor in place. I want to know how the baby is dealing with the stress."

Nick flinched. He'd forgotten about the baby's health in his worry over Faith. It would destroy her if she lost her sister's baby.

But it would destroy him if he lost *her*. Nick swallowed hard. How had it happened? When the hell had he fallen for this woman? Somehow she'd become a part of his life—a part of his heart. Even if she never returned his feelings, he wanted to know she woke up each morning, somewhere.

A technician slipped into the room and handed a folder to Dr. Grant.

Nick stepped forward. "How's it look?"

"Do you love your wife, Mr. Harrison?"

Nick nodded grimly. He didn't like the sound of this.

"Do you feel you can speak for her? For her best interests?"

Hesitating a second, he nodded again.

Dr. Grant turned to the nurse. "I'll need surgery one prepped. See if Dr. Lewis is still in the building to assist. Dr. Riley can anesthetize." He glanced toward Faith. "Have a pediatric ICU team onsite."

"What the hell is going on?" Nick demanded. Things were spiraling faster than he could follow.

"Come with me, I need to scrub. I can explain while we walk."

Nick was torn. He didn't want to leave Faith, but he needed to find out what was happening. After brushing a kiss on her forehead, he reluctantly followed the doctor.

"How serious is this?"

"All indications are that your wife has suffered placental separation. I'm judging it to be in the moderate to severe range."

Nick thought he understood so far.

"Your wife and the baby are both hemorrhaging. She's already lost at least a pint of blood. The situation is critical." Dr. Grant stopped him outside the door marked "surgical prep." "I'll need you to sign a waiver and make a choice."

"A choice?" Nick's voice struggled past his tight vocal chords. Nausea rose in the back of his throat.

"There is great risk involved. I need to know your priority. And Faith's. If the situation deteriorates, shall we focus on your wife or the baby?"

Nick stared at the man. Surely he must have misunderstood. He was supposed to choose between his brother's child and the woman he realized held his heart? What the hell kind of choice was that?

He swallowed the fear and panic threatening to take over—

there was really nothing to decide. Precious seconds were ticking.

"Faith." Nick's voice was firm with certainty.

Dr. Grant clapped a hand on his shoulder and disappeared through the doors.

Nick stared at the wall. He knew Faith would want the baby chosen, but he couldn't do it. He loved her too damn much to let her die. Defeated, he turned away feeling more alone than at any time in his miserable life.

Mab waited two feet behind him. Tears shimmered in her eyes. She'd heard and wrapped him in a brusque hug. "I'm proud of you. You made a choice that would have paralyzed most people and you made it with your heart."

He accepted her warmth for only a moment before he pulled back. "She'll never forgive me if she loses the baby."

Time stood still. And, yet, it rushed by faster than a runaway horse. No word came from Dr. Grant or the surgical team. Nick paced to the waiting room window again. He spun expectantly when a hand rested on his shoulder.

Logan.

He wasn't sure if he should be relieved it wasn't Dr. Grant or not. He returned his brother's firm handshake.

"Any word?"

"None." Nick muttered and resumed pacing. "Why is it taking so long?"

"You never helped a mare through a difficult birth?" Logan's voice trailed off. "Hang in there."

Logan approached Mab and settled into the seat next to her. They conversed in low whispers.

Nick turned back to the windows. All of these years he'd refused to acknowledge that love between a man and woman was possible. Now that he knew otherwise, it might be too late. Why hadn't he figured it out before now? What if he lost her?

I swear if Faith and the baby pull through, I'll leave them alone. If that's what she wants.

"Nick." Logan's voice attracted his attention.

He turned to see an exhausted Dr. Grant standing in the doorway. Nick tried to read the expression on his face. His heartbeat paused then resumed as the sheen of sweat broke out on his face.

The doctor moved toward him. Nick met him halfway. He ran a hand around the back of his stiff neck.

"Faith is going to be fine." Dr. Grant offered a weary smile. "I won't lie to you, it was touch and go for a while. But she's one strong lady."

Nick's shoulder's sagged with relief. *Thank you, God.* Then he tensed again. "The baby?" He saw Mab and Logan approach.

Dr. Grant's smile covered his face. "A fighter like his mother. He'll be in the ICU for observation for a couple of hours."

"A boy?" Nick didn't trust he'd understood correctly. "They both made it?" Joy spread through his limbs.

"If all goes well, a few days recovery and they'll be fine." Dr. Grant accepted Nick and Logan's handshakes before he left.

Logan and Mab congratulated him as Nick pasted a smile on his face. He'd made a bargain with fate and it was time to pay. He'd have to let Faith go. There was no other choice. She meant too much to him.

Nick slipped from the room while the others talked. He needed to get back to the ranch. It was time to call his lawyer.

Faith fixed her gaze on Logan. He stood next to her hospital bed and shuffled his boots.

"Has Nick even seen the baby?"

The question forced him to meet her eyes. "No. He left as soon as he knew you and the baby were out of danger."

"I don't understand." She pushed against the pillows plumped behind her back. A pain from her incision site reminded her again of the miracle that had arrived in the form of a healthy baby boy.

Only Nick's quick actions had saved her life. As well as the baby's.

Logan pulled a chair next to the bed. He settled into it and twisted his hat in his nervous fingers. His gaze remained on the floor between his feet.

"What's going on?" Faith needed answers. She was thrilled about the baby, but her happiness was marred by Nick's continued absence.

Logan looked up. "What do you remember about what happened after you arrived at the hospital?"

"Nothing, I woke up in recovery. You and Mab were there, but not Nick."

He hesitated before continuing. "Has Dr. Grant mentioned the waivers Nick had to sign?"

"Not that I remember." Faith wrinkled her forehead. "The standard admission forms?"

"Not…exactly."

Faith held her hands up and glared at him. "Spit it out. I'm a big girl. I can take it."

"You know, I think you can." He flashed a rare smile. "While you were rushed into surgery, Dr. Grant asked Nick to set the surgical priority."

She tilted her head in confusion. "I don't understand."

Logan stood and paced to the foot of the bed before he continued. "Nick was forced to choose between you and the baby. *If* a decision had to be made by the surgical team on life-saving priority."

Faith shuddered. "Oh, no. Poor Nick."

He came around the side of the bed and stared at her. "Aren't you interested in his decision?"

"It isn't important. Family comes first and he shouldn't have been forced to make such a decision. He knew the baby was my priority. I understand—"

"No, I don't think you do." He leaned closer and placed a hand on either side of her shoulders, ensuring direct eye contact while he spoke. "He chose you, Faith. Not his brother's child. You."

She shook her head as his final word reverberated in her heart. It couldn't possibly be true, but she saw the truth reflected in Logan's steady gaze. "Why?"

He straightened and shrugged. "I think you can come up with an answer yourself. I've butted in enough to have Nick knock me on my backside a dozen times over." Brushing a fleeting kiss on her forehead, he turned and disappeared through the door.

She stared at the closed door after he'd left.

Nick chose me, dear God, he chose me.

She smiled as a lone tear slid over her cheek.

Faith checked her face in the mirror one more time. Mab had jumped at the chance to help her apply some subtle makeup and arrange her hair in loose curls and tendrils. Faith shuffled back to the bed, sore from standing so long.

Easing down onto the mattress, she carefully arranged herself for maximum effect. If Wayne managed his part, Nick would arrive any moment. Logan waited in the nursery, prepared to have the baby delivered to the room at the right time.

Faith drew a shaky breath. Maybe this wasn't a good idea. She was scared. Terrified. Her entire future hinged on the next few minutes. Not to mention her heart. It was a gamble, but she knew she needed to risk everything if she hoped for a chance at a future with Nick. She had to risk it all if she wanted it all.

A soft knock sent her heart crashing against her rib cage. "Come in."

Nick pushed the door open and warily stepped into the room. He didn't meet her gaze.

"How are you?" Faith's question seemed to catch him by surprise.

"I think that's my line." He smiled, stepping a foot closer.

She searched her suddenly blank mind for a topic of conversation. "Any permanent damage to your truck?"

"Taken care of." Nick laughed. No sign of those irresistible dimples, but it was a start.

"Good." Faith groaned inside. They sounded like polite strangers.

"Wayne mentioned there was a problem with paperwork."

He broached the excuse she'd used to lure him to the hospital.

"Not exactly." Faith glanced at the door. Where was Logan?

As if on cue, the door swung open. The charge nurse pushed a bassinet next to the bed. "This little man thinks it's time to eat. Again. He has quite an appetite." She glanced at Nick. "He'll end up as tall as his daddy."

"Thank you for bringing him." The door closed softly as the nurse left. They were alone with the baby.

Faith leaned over and winced.

Nick was beside her in a second. "What's wrong?"

"I'm okay." She settled against the pillows. "The cesarean stitches pull when I bend. Could you lift him up to me?"

She pretended not to see the panic on Nick's face as his gaze darted from the baby to the door and back again. Cautiously, he reached into the bassinet.

Faith smothered a laugh. "He's much tougher than he looks."

Nick lifted the baby into his strong arms and studied the tiny face. "Strong like his mother. What did you name him?"

"I wanted to wait for you before making it official."

His eyes remained focused on the squirming body cradled in his arms and softness changed the contours of his rugged face.

Faith smiled. "I thought Steven Nicholas would be appropriate."

Nick's attention focused on her for a moment, before returning to the baby. "If you're sure."

"I'm sure." She slipped the top two buttons of her gown loose. "Looks like little Steven is hungry." She tried not to feel self-conscious about the swell of her breast being exposed.

Nick awkwardly held the baby toward her.

"Can you lay him on my lap, please?"

He moved closer and his eyes lingered on her flesh. He leaned down to place Steven on her lap. When he pulled back, Faith took a deep breath and grasped Nick's fingers. With a gentle tug she managed to have him sit on the edge of the bed near her hip.

Gathering her nerve, she brushed the gown aside and helped the baby find what he was seeking. The heat of Nick's gaze burned her skin. "He has ten fingers and ten toes."

"He's perfect." Nick's hushed words drew Faith's attention. "Thank you."

Faith didn't look away this time, but met his gaze. "For what?"

"For being gutsy enough to do something like this for Carrie and Steve."

"When you love someone, you do anything for them. You don't count the cost to yourself." Faith didn't understand the frown that her words brought to his face.

Nick stood and stared down at her. "I've instructed my attorney to draft annulment papers." He watched the greedy infant suckle for a moment. "There won't be a custody battle. I hope I can be a part of Steven's life, somehow."

Faith's eyes widened. She'd misread the signs. Perhaps his choice before the surgery meant something other than she hoped. Maybe, Nick didn't have feelings for her. At least, not the same ones she had for him. A small part of her heart withered.

"Why? I thought..." She couldn't form a coherent thought, much less a sentence.

Nick took another step toward the door and away from her. "The marriage was a bad idea. I had no right to threaten you into it. I was wrong and I'm sorry."

I'm losing him. Had she ever had him?

"The papers will be delivered this afternoon." He placed his hand on the doorknob.

Don't let him open the door and walk out of your life.

"Nick?"

He looked at her, his eyes unreadable and his jaw tight.

Faith had to know his reason. "Why?"

"Why, what?" He looked cornered and desperate to escape the room.

She cleared her throat. "Why did you choose *me?*"

Nick didn't pretend to misunderstand. She noticed the vein pulsing at his temple as his hand dropped from the knob, but feared that he wouldn't explain.

Instead of leaving, he walked to the side of the bed and watched the baby for a moment. He reached his hand down and the back of one knuckle stroked little Steven's cheek. The tip of Nick's finger brushed Faith's skin and lingered.

"Nick?" The word was a breathless plea.

"I'm no good with words and saying what needs to be said." His eyes searched hers.

Faith removed the sleeping infant from her nipple, leaned sideways and placed him in the bassinet. She pulled her gown closed, but left it unbuttoned.

Nick swallowed. "I don't know how to love you the way you deserve. I don't know how to tell you…"

Reaching out, she circled his large wrist with her fingers. She pulled until he surrendered and sat next to her.

Nick opened his mouth to speak. She pressed her other hand against his warm lips to silence the words.

"If you can't tell me…" She laced her hands behind his neck and lowered his mouth toward hers. "Show me."

Logan eased Faith's door closed. He turned to face a grinning Mab. Wayne and Emily waited nearby.

He and Mab exchanged a triumphant high-five.

Thank God a Harrison male finally had the good sense to accept the love offered to him. Their mother's legacy was over.

A new legacy was born.

Harlequin Romance®

is thrilled to present a lively new trilogy from

Jessica Hart:

City Brides

*They're on the career ladder,
but just one step away from the altar!*

Meet Phoebe, Kate and Bella...

These friends suddenly realize that they're fast approaching thirty and haven't yet found Mr. Right—or even Mr. Maybe!

But that's about to change. If fate won't lend a hand, they'll make their own luck. Whether it's a hired date or an engagement of convenience, they're determined that the next wedding invitation they see will be one of their own!

July—
FIANCÉ WANTED FAST!
(#3757)

August—
THE BLIND-DATE PROPOSAL
(#3761)

September—
THE WHIRLWIND ENGAGEMENT
(#3765)

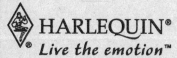

HARLEQUIN®
Live the emotion™

Visit us at www.eHarlequin.com

HRCBJH3T

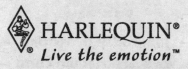

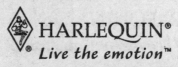

Harlequin Romance®

is delighted to present a brand-new miniseries
that dares to be different...

TANGO

FRESH AND FLIRTY...
IT TAKES TWO TO TANGO

Exuberant, exciting...emotionally exhilarating!

These cutting-edge, highly contemporary stories
capture how women in the twenty-first century
really feel about meeting Mr. Right!

Don't miss:

July:
MANHATTAN MERGER
—by international bestselling
author Rebecca Winters (#3755)

October:
THE BABY BONDING
—by rising star
Caroline Anderson (#3769)

November:
THEIR ACCIDENTAL BABY
—by fresh new talent
Hannah Bernard (#3774)

And watch for more
TANGO books to come!

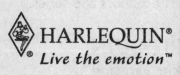

HARLEQUIN®
Live the emotion™

Visit us at www.eHarlequin.com   HRTANGJ3